VILLA LEILA

A MUDDY TALE OF LOVE & MONSTERS

ADAM HERMAN

Teal Island

This book is a work of fiction. The characters, incidents, and dialogue are drawn from the author's imagination and are not to be construed as real. Any resemblance to actual persons or events is entirely coincidental.

ISBN-13: 979-8-9868675-1-9

To my hometown.

THE CREATURE FROM THE MISSISSIPPI

ONE

Fate has a heavy hand. She aims with perfect intention, but throws with imperfect form. Maybe she had been drinking. Or maybe, just maybe, she hadn't been drinking enough. Sometimes a little buzz helps find the sweet spot you need. Before you know it, you're in the zone and throwing one hell of a game of darts. That is, until that third shot of Fireball arrives at the table. You didn't order it, but there it is regardless, luring you in with its sweet song. All of a sudden, your girlfriend of eight months starts smoking again, you've agreed to go camping with some strangers, and your phone is cracked and dead.

Perfect intention, however, does not equate perfect outcome. This is the thorn in her side, Fate's. She tries and tries and tries and yet, somehow, free will comes along and finds a way to screw things up for her.

But life is full of endless wonder, and, once in a rare while, Fate hits a bull's-eye... and that, my friends, is where the real magic happens.

****

It was morning and the river was alive. Her current, usually gentle and easy, was now roaring along through the heartland, cutting the western border of Illinois from the eastern border of Missouri. It was a brisk fall morning, and the water was high this time of year. August had seen more than enough rain to make up for the dry summer, and, for the first time in a while, the farmers had very little to complain about. The sun was shining as its light danced on the water's surface. There was an easy breeze; a perfect day on the big Mississippi.

A pair of bald eagles were perched high among the white oak trees on the Missouri side of the water. Their hungry eyes scanned the muddy river. There was a nest next to them with some newly hatched babies who were ready for breakfast. The fast moving current pushed most of the menu into shallower waters, closer to the bank; and there, on the eastern side of Whitney Island, they saw their prey.

The flicker of light reflected off the side of a smallmouth bass, as he snapped at a dragonfly. This was their chance. The male eagle spread his wings and hit the air fast, beginning his descent. The mother stood by to protect the babies from any threats in the area. Her stomach rumbled with the thought of fresh fish. She was a pickier eater than her mate. She preferred fish over all but was not opposed to the occasional treat: small reptiles, rabbits, squirrels. Her partner and the father of her newly hatched children, was a far less picky eater. He would consume anything he could get his talons on. The Mississippi was always full of garbage, and there were more than enough choices for him to try. He had eaten glass bottles, pieces of fishing poles, old beer cans. There was one time when he even ate a dog's squeak toy. It was just sitting there on the river bank, and he thought it was a chipmunk. He never could digest it quite right, and still, sometimes when he turned to the left he squeaked. Whatever. It's all good.

The father eagle flew over the smallmouth and turned to face the wind as he made his approach to the water's surface. The bass was motionless. *This is too easy!* He neared the water and reached out with his right talon, making contact with the fish. As he began to pump his wings and fly away, he felt some resistance. He flapped his wings harder as he looked down. His talon was stuck below the water, something clamped down on it!

The water began to churn, and before he knew what was happening, he saw something sharp. *What in tarnation is...* His thoughts were interrupted by an enormous splash as a creature the size of a man broke through the surface and grabbed him, bringing him underwater in one swift movement! A single feather floated in the air, and the creature had vanished back below, a quiet squeaking noise fading along with it.

The smallmouth bass didn't even notice because he's just a stupid ass fish.

TWO

The restaurant was noisy. The sounds of knives and forks banging together in syncopated rhythms sounded like some underpaid salsa band that hadn't eaten in days. Theo and his eight year old daughter sat in silence. She had her nose to her menu, coloring away furiously. He stared out the boring window at his boring town, bored with the boringness of it all. A very tall waiter approached them. His forearms were covered in tattoos, while the rest of him, Theo figured, was probably not.

"Have we reached a verdict?" the young waiter asked, with a hint of "whoa" in his voice. The only thing missing was a hair flip.

"Saylor?" Theo asked his daughter, interrupting the creative genius that most eight year olds possess, before the world strips it away from them slowly and cruelly, conformity its dull tool.

"Grilled cheese and veggies," she answered without looking up.

"Are you sure you don't want to switch it up? Fortune favors the bold, ya know. Why not try something new?" Theo said.

"Nah," she answered.

"Okay, she'll have the grilled cheese..."

"With veggies," Saylor added.

"Yes, with veggies," Theo said, looking back at the open menu.

"And I'll have..." Theo took a moment to scan the menu one last time.

Saylor sighed and looked up dramatically, her head cocked to the side. She looked at the waiter. "He'll have the Reuben," she said with confidence.

"Yeah, I'll have a Reuben, please," Theo answered. He closed the menu and handed it to him. The waiter didn't bother writing anything down and strutted away.

"You know you should try new things, Dad. Fortune's flavor is bold, ya know," she mimicked him as she resumed her coloring.

Theo smiled. These were the rare times he enjoyed not working. He had spent the last twelve years as a fire-fighter for the city of Chicago, Illinois, and had loved almost every minute of it, but he never truly felt at home here. In fact, he had never really felt at home anywhere. If you were to ask him where he was from he would answer: "I was born in a small town on the Mississippi River called Kenton, Illinois, but I got out of there as fast as my legs could take me."

Kenton, Illinois, was a town full of lost causes, ignored history and unappreciated beauty. The few original districts of the town were built upon a rich past with incredibly ornate architecture. There were stories behind those buildings.

The town began as a shelter for the Potawatomi tribe during their forced relocation from Indiana to Kansas. The tribe soon found themselves sharing the shelter with members of the Church of Jesus Christ of Latter-day Saints, after being kicked out of Missouri by the state militia during the Missouri-Mormon War of 1838. Then, in the 1840's, German migrants began to settle in Kenton, escaping the revolutions between the provinces in Germany and greater European conflicts. With them they brought beautiful architecture, great beer, and cows... a shitload of cows.

Immigrants from New England began to make their way south to Kenton with their progressive values and their ideas of abolitionism. Kenton began to grow into a major hub for the Underground Railroad. It seemed as if it were a welcome home for the persecuted. The unwelcome of all kinds were knocking on Kenton's door. (Until many years later, denim clad high-schoolers would be smoking Pall Malls in the gravel parking lot outside of Kenton High School, waiting impatiently to get the hell out of this dead-end town. Go Wildcats!) These days Kenton was full of the prematurely cynical.

Eventually, the steamboats came and bridges were built and life on the river was lucrative and good. Businesses were booming, and the population grew.

Theo paid the check, stood up, and helped his daughter with her jacket. He thanked the hostess as they walked out into the foyer. He held the door open for his daughter while she walked under his arm, playing a game on his phone. It was either the one about some pissed off birds or the one where she bakes a cake. They walked slowly toward his old pickup truck. Theo did his best to hide his limp. The phone rang, interrupting her game.

"Unknown number," she said.

"Oh?! A spam risk is it?! I'm sure this is important," he said to Saylor as she handed him his phone. Theo answered, "City morgue, you kill 'em we chill 'em!"

"Hello, is this Mr. Beckett?" A woman responded.

"Maybe. Who be calling my phone?" Theo winked at his daughter. She rolled her eyes.

"This is Melinda Roberts. I'm the nurse at your father's hospice," the woman said on the other end of the line.

Theo didn't know how to respond. *Hospice*? He had known that his father was sick, but he didn't realize that he had been put into hospice. It had been a while since they had last spoken, and those were apathetic words at best. He wanted his daughter to have a relationship with her grandfather, but he was always at bay. He wasn't the type of person to let some kid into his life, even if it was his own flesh and blood.

"Look, I didn't realize that...," he started.

"I'm sorry to say that it looks like it may be time to say goodbye," she said. She had kindness in her voice that seemed natural, unlike some of the well-versed hospital staff he had known in the past. "How soon can you get here?"

Theo looked at his watch. "I'm four-ish hours from Kenton. I have to drop my daughter off with her mom," he looked at Saylor. She noticed the tone switch in his voice and had a look of concern in her eyes. He ruffled her hair in a playful manner in an attempt to hide the seriousness of things. "I guess I could get there by five," he said.

"Okay," she answered. "Let's hope he can hold on until then."

Theo thanked her and hung up the phone.

"Is everything alright?" Saylor asked him.

"Right as rain, Daughter," Theo said, lying to them both. "Right as rain."

THREE

Theo walked into the small room and broke the heavy silence. Hospice seemed like a dream. His father lay in bed, unconscious and breathing deeply. Melinda greeted him at the door and showed him to his father. Abner Beckett was lying on his back. He was breathing, but it wasn't his breath anymore. It was just movement of air at this point. A machine beeped slowly as Theo approached the bedside and looked down. He stood there for a moment, collecting his thoughts.

"So this is it," he said to no one in particular.

"Is there anything I can get for you? Some water maybe?" Melinda asked him.

"No, thank you," Theo answered even though he was thirsty.

"I'll give you a minute with him," Melinda said, before leaving the room.

Theo stood in silence, watching his father breathe. Thoughts of his childhood crept into his mind. He remembered watching his father working in the garage, desperate for his attention. Attention that his father was rarely one to give. He was cold and hardened; an icy planet of a man, deep in the edges of the solar system. He gave more affection to the fishing pole he was working on.

"Come on..," he said to his father. A heart rate monitor beeped slowly. "I know you can hear me in there," Theo continued. "Come on, give me something."

"I haven't asked for anything from you in a very long time. I'm asking now. Just one thing. I don't want an apology. Just something that I can hold on to that proves you aren't a total ass. You've made it very clear, over the years, that you don't give a shit about me."

The beeping continued.

"I don't need any wisdom. I don't need an 'I love you, Son.' I just need something I can give to your granddaughter so that she can hold on to it and not think of her grandfather as a lonely old prick, who wasted his life away." Melinda walked back into the room and stood in the corner. Theo ignored her. He was desperate, but determined not to show it. "Please," he said, under his breath.

To Theo's surprise, his father moved. He lifted a shaking left hand and placed it on the right side of his chest, slowly. The breathing stopped. The heart rate monitor went flat. The beeping turned into a tiny siren. Abner Beckett had died. Theo let out a frustrated sigh.

The nurse walked over and turned off the heart rate monitor. "I'm very sorry for your loss, Theo," she said.

"Don't be," Theo said as he left the room.

FOUR

The sun set on Kenton as Theo drove to his father's house. The radio scanned the available stations, giving a five-second preview to each overplayed song, but nothing felt right to stop the scan and listen to in full. He rolled the window down and let the cool air in. He thought that this would have hit faster. Emotions weren't flooding into him all at once, but they were beginning to seep in slowly. He needed a drink. Fortunately, Kenton was well equipped for drinking. There was a bar on every corner in this town, but tonight he needed to drink alone.

He pulled into the driveway next to his dad's old 1967 Chevy C/K truck. He stepped out of his car and saw the porch lights on across the street. It was Heather, Abner's neighbor and Theo's childhood friend. She was sitting on her front steps, smoking a joint. There was a giant cactus plant sitting next to her. Theo and Heather had been close friends since grade school. The two of them trusted each other more than anyone else. When the house across the street from Theo's childhood home went up for sale, she couldn't resist moving in.

"THEOOOOO!" she yelled from across the street. Theo stepped out of his truck and crossed to join her. Crickets and bullfrogs came to life and began to sing. Summer was still holding on by a thread.

Heather sat cross-legged on the first step to her porch. She wore all black, with black lipstick, and dyed black hair. Her big, round eyes contrasted her small petite face. She looked as though she could see it all. She got it. She had been awoken, but would now rather still be asleep like the rest of the herd; an empath in a mean old world.

"Hey, lady," Theo said as he sat down next to her and nodded toward the cactus. "New roommate?"

"Yep. This is Stevie Pricks. I won her in a staring contest. I beat three people in a row, all in the same round." She handed him the joint. Theo pretended to take a hit. He was never a big weed guy. "I'm sorry about your dad," she said.

"Thanks, I guess. I'm not really sure how to feel about it. He was an ass," Theo responded.

"Yeah, but he still died." She took the joint back, "Lucky bastard."

"Don't worry, Heather. You'll be marching towards that dark eternity soon, too."

"Hell yeah," she responded through a cough, "Sounds dope." They shared a laugh together. "How's it feel to be an orphan?" she asked.

"I don't know if I can still be an orphan at thirty-six. Does that still count?" Theo asked.

"Yeah, that counts." Heather answered. She handed the joint back to Theo.

"Feels about the same, I guess. Not like he was around much anyway." Theo took a hit and accidentally inhaled more than he had planned. "I'm just worried about how Saylor is going to take it. She has the biggest heart I've ever seen."

"You've got one, too... somewhere in that stuffy chest of yours." she said as she gave him a small shoulder bump. It made him cough. Heather laughed.

Heather had dreamed of becoming an apothecary. She wanted to mix herbs and chemicals and magic and ease people's suffering. She wanted to help people sleep and dream. She wanted to battle people's anxieties with her bare hands in the soil.

After enrolling in an herbalism school in southern Illinois, she found herself drawn toward the chemistry of medicine. She transferred to another university closer to home and became a pharmacist. She worked for years at the local pharmacy, and as time went on she saw more and more into the medicine business and realized that she and big pharma just didn't share the same values. She was put on this planet to help others, not just herself. So she quit. She saved up some money and took out a loan and opened a small bookstore. But the desire to heal never went away.

Theo continued, "I guarantee he treated my mom like dirt. He was always so cold and distant. I don't know... maybe he tried, in his own way I guess... maybe. I just want to get all of this behind me. I'm going to clean out his garage this weekend, then see the lawyers and figure out wha..."

"Theo, I know that this is hard for you in a weird way," Heather interrupted, "but to be fair, how do you know that he treated your mother poorly? She died when you were born..."

"How could he not have?! I just know. He was so cold, Heather. No one with that little interest in his family could have treated his wife well. It's just obvious... I mean... he was so lost inside wherever he was... I don't know." Theo was feeling the buzz.

He stood up from the steps. He was tired. "I'm gonna get some sleep. I think I got accidentally stoned," Theo said. "Let's catch up tomorrow?"

Heather smiled, her dark lips contrasted against her pale face in the moonlight. Theo walked away toward his late father's dark house.

"Hey wait! You know what would cheer you up?!" Heather yelled after him. "Chicken Wiggles!"

"No. Heather, I don't have time for Chicken Wiggles right now. I'm sorry," Theo yelled back to her.

"Come on! We never play Chicken Wiggles anymore," Heather yelled through cupped her hands around her mouth. Chicken Wiggles was a childhood game that could only be understood by witnessing. It was a special celebration that could only be pulled out in the most important of situations. The first time that they played Chicken Wiggles, and possibly its inception, was when Heather won the spelling bee in the third grade. It became a part of their life ever since. From moments like getting their driver's licenses, to Theo losing his virginity, to Heather opening her bookstore, Chicken Wiggles had been there.

"My dad just died! I can't play Chicken Wiggles!" Theo yelled back. A light came on in the house next door.

"You just said you didn't care!"

"I'm an orphan!"

"Oh, poor Theo! 'Stead of treated, you get tricked?! You know what? Go fuck yourself then!" Heather yelled across the way.

"Goodnight, Heather," Theo yelled to her. He spun toward the next door neighbors. "And goodnight to you, Mr. and Mrs. Miller!"

Theo laughed to himself as their curtains shut, and the windows darkened. *Maybe Dad had some wine,* he thought as he unlocked the front door.

FJVE

The Villa Leila stood alone upon the bluffs, overlooking the banks of the Mississippi River. The Moroccan castle appeared like something out of a mirage, contrasting the American Midwest in the background. Its strong pise foundation held four stories above it, each with beautiful, bell shaped windows placed evenly throughout the clay walls. It was built for a happily-ever-after that was stolen away, and had since been unoccupied for almost fifty years. The traditional riad design held the remains of a fountain in the middle courtyard that had long stopped working, and the once lavish reflecting pool was now filled with concrete. If not for the Kenton Historical Society stepping in, the building would have easily fallen into disrepair at the hands of stoned teenagers and the assholery of squirrels and other such rodents. The money made from the weekend tours was just enough to retain the home's elegance, and the time spent in ruin was just enough to retain its mystery.

Theo had taken his daughter on a tour of the villa one weekend, and Saylor instantly fell in love with the story behind the haunted home. She would share it with anyone who would listen, but the story always seemed to change.

"It all began with Mr. Gray Dougal," she would tell her captivated classmates during recess. "He was a wealthy artist-cat and loved to travel and had many,

many adventures. On one particular adventure, Gray's camel died, and he was stranded and lost in the Sahara Desert. It was so hot during the day that he would wait until the sun went down and follow the stars in the night sky, hoping to be rescued. He walked for three nights until he found his way to a small village in Morocco, called Merzouga. The people there were barbers."

"Barbers?" one of the children asked.

"Yes, this village had the best hair in all of Morocco," Saylor continued, "Anyway, Gray was so happy to have found people, and he was finally saved. Then something unexpected happened. He met the most beautiful woman he had ever seen, and he fell in love with her. Her name was Leila, and she fell in love with him, too!"

Another student jumped in and interrupted, "They weren't allowed to be together because they had different religions, so they kept it a secret. When her father found out…"

"Who's telling the story here, Kenzie?" Saylor said sternly, her hands in the air. "So like I was saying, "Saylor continued, keeping her eyes fixed on Kenzie, "they weren't allowed to be together because they came from different places, but love has no boundaries, and they decided to run away together.

"They knew that the only way to escape was to leave in the middle of the night, so they packed their things and snuck away under a moonless eve…" Saylor would really get into the story at this point, "and headed north towards the Mediterranean Sea, where a fairy took them to Spain."

"No, not a fairy! It was a genie," Kenzie said.

"Genies aren't real!" Saylor responded. "Anyway, they headed north to escape, but they had to split up…"

"My dad said that Gray and his best friend, Carson, went there to find a hidden treasure and that they found a magic lamp. And that's how he got all his money!" another student added.

"See?" Kenzie said. She felt vindication. Saylor rolled her eyes in annoyance. "That's ridiculous. This story is about love, not magic treasure," Saylor said.

"Maybe he wished for Leila to be in love with him?" the other student said.

"No," Saylor answered. "You can't wish to make someone love you. It's against genie rules."

"So you're admitting that genies exist!" Kenzie said. She finally had her on the ropes.

"Can we get back to the story?" Saylor said.

"Yeah! Then what happened?" another student asked.

"After they split up, Gray made his way back to America and came home to Kenton. He wanted to surprise his love when she arrived. He thought he would build her a place to live to remind her of home, so he built the Villa Leila. He waited and waited, but still Leila never arrived. Days turned into weeks, weeks turned into months, months turned into years, and still no sign of Leila. He wrote letter after letter after letter, but never heard back. Eventually, Gray hid himself away from the world and became a recluse in Villa Leila. His only companion was his dog, Cheddar. He never knew what happened to his Leila, and eventually he died of a broken heart."

"So sad," one of the third graders responded. A few sniffles in the crowd followed.

"Some even say that the ghost of Cheddar still wanders the grounds!" Saylor added.

"That's not true!" Kenzie would jump back in, "My mom told me that they all lived happily ever after."

"Well your mother is wrong, and your family sleeps in a bed of lies," Saylor replied.

The legend of Villa Leila: romantic. The design: beautiful. The mystery: haunting. And less than a mile away from this delicate and beautiful structure stood another Kenton staple and more popular date destination, Uncle Jim's Beer and Bait. What an amazing world that we live in.

SIX

Damian sat at the edge of the bar, drunk. He was a regular patron at the Cherry Street Tavern. The bar was painfully slow for a Thursday night, and his chances of meeting a lady were slim to none, but Damian was too drunk to feel down about it. It was almost midnight, and the dreaded 'last call' was nigh. An old blues song drifted softly from the jukebox. The neon lights bathed the wooden tables in red. Old photographs and vintage beer signs were hung with very little care all around the small bar. It was as if Time, himself, had forgotten about the place and left it to drift through the sands alone.

"Hey, honey," Damian called out to the bartender, "I'll have another."

The bartender approached him from the other side of the bar. She was in her early twenties, and although she had grown used to sleazy patrons calling her 'honey' or 'darling,' she still had no patience for it. The tips were decent, and the hours worked with her school schedule, and where else could she work in a town like Kenton and make the same kind of money? She decided that she would take her chances with the drunks. And Damian was a drunk's drunk. The kind of drunk that made other drunks feel better about themselves. She disliked him and didn't care if he knew it.

"What did you say, Damian? You want something for the last call?" she asked, devoid of emotion.

"Yeah, I'll take my regular," he slurred back.

"What's your 'regular'?"

"You know what I like, baby girl. Come on! My regular drink." He looked around incredulously.

"The only 'regular' drink you have is whatever someone else is buying," she snapped back. "And if you call me 'baby girl' or 'honey' again, I'll slam your head into that bar that you're drooling on so hard you'll be shitting splinters. We're closing down." She walked away and began ringing a bell that hung above the cash register. "LAST CALL. Finish 'em up, ya'll!"

Damian began shuffling around for his coat and searching for his keys in his pocket. His money fell to the floor, and he bent down to pick it all up.

Damian was in his late forties, and was not aging well. He would smoke every cigarette that he could find, and he would drink on most days like he was about to lose a foot from the Civil War. You could barely make out the fading 'River Rat' tattoo through the leathery skin on his left shoulder. He worked as a welder for a private company that built boat trailers, and got as much joy out of it as one could imagine. His divorce from years ago had cost him most of his retirement and a small house, so he had been living in an elevated river camp on the banks of the Mississippi ever since.

He sat back at the bar to finish what was left of his warm beer. "Hey, sugar…" he called back over to the bartender. She turned around and began walking toward him. Her eyes lit up with rage.

"I just wanted to say that I think you should smile more. I didn't mean anyth..." He was interrupted by the sound of his own face smacking wood, as she dribbled his head off the bar like a basketball. The force was strong enough that he bounced back from it and fell to the floor. The sound of the thud and rattled glasses rang out in the quiet bar. The few patrons remaining fearfully added a couple bucks to their tips before scurrying out the back door, lest that be their fate someday.

Damian's vision refocused as he picked himself off of the floor again. He counted his money through the stars he was seeing and left what he thought was a good tip on the bar before staggering outside.

The stars were bright, and the air was thick as he began his regular journey home. He was a little over a mile from the river bank where he lived, but the drunken zig zag added at least another fifty yards to the distance.

"Typical woman," he muttered to himself as he approached a bush on the corner of the sidewalk.

"Ungrateful she-devils!" He reached into the bush and pulled out a lukewarm can of beer.

Some people build bridges through the wisdom of engineering. Some people create medicines and vaccines through the diablerie of science. We live in a world of genius and innovation. Damian would walk to the bar after he got off of work and would leave himself cans of beer for the walk home. He called them his "bush lights." This was his gift. It was like a fun little trail of crumbs leading him back to his river camp. But instead of this redneck Hansel getting baked in an oven, he would get baked on some cheap weed in a plastic bong that was given to him by his neighbor. River rats gotta stick together.

The rumbling of the Mississippi grew louder as he approached the gravel road that led to his elevated camp. Flood season was over, and the dry gravel was dusty this time of the year. In an effort to avoid water damage, houses on the river banks were often built on tall stilts with stairways up to the doors. Damian bought this particular river camp years ago, back when he was in love and he knew happiness by a first name. It would be a place that he and his wife could spend the weekends fishing and boating and just watching the river go by.

Since his wife left him, however, both he and his river camp had fallen into disrepair. Once his divorce was finalized, he decided to have a drink. Then he had another. And another. Then he thought, *why quit now*? And Damian, the River Rat, just kept on drinking. He gave up on love and gave up on health and accepted his fate as an aging tradesman. He would circle the drain in a Van Halen t-shirt and a pair of cut-off jeans.

There was only one thing left in this world that Damian loved, and that was a big dumb turtle named Gustav. Damian found Gustav sitting on top of a fence post. He was on his way to work when he saw him. Some awful human had placed the turtle on top of the post on his belly where his legs could do nothing but dangle. He was left there to his fate. Gustav just sat there, maybe for days, praying for a wind strong enough to tip him off.

He never would have thought that his salvation would come in the form of a very hung over divorcee in an old rusty pickup truck, but luck has endless forms, and the two had been best friends ever since.

The moonlight illuminated the old wooden stairs that led to the only door on the house. The porch light had been burned out for a year now, and Damian didn't mind it. The only other things that ever used it were the moths. The old porch faced east, maybe twenty feet from the bank of the river. The sunsets over the water were beautiful, but Damian hadn't seen one in years. He was usually at the bar by then. He stumbled up the stairs, muttering a song to himself, and didn't hear the strange rumbling from the shallow waters below. It sounded like a low growl.

He fumbled the keys before opening the door. He turned on the light and was greeted by Gustav.

"Hey there, buddy. How's my man?" He slurred to the turtle before making kissy sounds. Gustav looked up at him and gave him an empty stare.

Damian walked towards the kitchenette and began to open a bag of turtle food. Gustav moved slowly yet eagerly. Damian bent down to give his buddy some dinner, but froze at the sound of a loud growling coming from outside. He turned slowly toward the front door, not quite paralyzed with fear, but close enough. There was something on his porch, a creature the size of a man, and it was staring right at him through the glass!

SEVEN

The smoke from the fire carried the scent of burning chemicals throughout the neighborhood. No one seemed to care, though, as that was a regular thing in Kenton. It was as if the community was saying, "Hey there, welcome to Kenton! Enjoy some complimentary emphysema. It's on the house!"

Theo didn't know what else to do with some of the junk he found in his father's garage, and he thought maybe a bonfire would be therapeutic. Most of the things were to be donated, but some of the random odds and ends were of use to no one. He tossed an old cardboard box that was full of older cardboard boxes on the fire. He couldn't help but feel it was a sort of funeral pyre to some of the memories that were swirling through his head.

He walked back into the garage and continued cleaning. There was an old tin sign doubling as a thermometer hanging on the wall. Theo figured that it hadn't been touched in fifteen years. A workbench blanketed in a thick layer of sawdust held various tools and wires. There was a corner of the garage dedicated to firewood and old lifejackets. Theo recognized one of them from his childhood. It was a small blue one with a cartoon dog on the back. Theo remembered begging his father to take him out on the boat when he would go. Abner always seemed disinterested and busy; however, once in a while he and Theo's uncle would go out on the river and check their trout lines.

The garage brought back a lot of memories for Theo, so he decided to be a typical dude and ignore the emotionally mature adult somewhere inside of him. He buried the feelings in a deep place, only to one day, possibly be resurfaced by an overpriced therapist who came to work barefoot.

"Let's check out the guest room," Theo said to the empty house. The sound of the closing door reverberated throughout the rooms. Theo put a record on his father's old turntable in an effort to drown out the quiet. He didn't expect the process to be so taxing. In an unplanned way, it made Theo resent his father a little bit more.

There wasn't much in the guest room, which wasn't really a guest room at all. It served as more of a storage room for Abner's fishing gear. There sat a full size bed near the far wall, with an old quilt folded over it. Theo never spent much time in this room as a kid, but something about it felt so welcoming and peaceful. For the first time since his arrival in Kenton, Theo felt at home.

He walked over to the desk near the closet and sat down. It was covered with fishing lures and lines, with the occasional beer can. A framed picture stood on the backside of the desk. It was of Abner and Theo when he was in the third grade. Standing next to it, was another picture of Theo's mother, when she was twenty-two, before Theo was born.

She was a beautiful woman, with dark brown hair, and green eyes that could cut right through you. Theo never knew her, but he always assumed they would be similar. There were nights, as a kid, when Abner would turn his attention away, that Theo would lie in bed and talk with his mother in the night. He would imagine what she would say back. He would laugh at the silly jokes she would make, and then he would laugh again after she would tickle him.

"Goodnight, Mom. I love you," he would say to the darkness. And, although there was usually no answer, he swore that sometimes he would hear an "I love you, Theo," coming from somewhere in the night.

Theo stared into the pictures until something caught his eye. A lone fishing rod was leaning into the corner, like it was wearing a leather jacket and smoking a cigarette in the school parking lot. Theo remembered this particular fishing rod. He remembered begging his father to take him with him, as Abner loaded the rod and reel into the back of his pick-up truck.

"I can't take you with me, Theo. This is a secret fishing spot. I can't take anyone there. Go help your grandmother," he would say.

Theo would sulk back into the house, helping his grandmother clear the table and do the dishes. The pain of rejection never truly healed.

Theo picked up the pole. *Fuck it. Let's go fishing.*

EJGHT

The humid air felt cool blowing across Theo's left arm as he let it hang out of the driver's side window. His right hand gripped the steering wheel loosely, guiding Abner's old pick-up truck down State Highway 57 toward Fall Creek. Fall Creek had no sign, nor could it be found on the GPS, but Theo knew where he was going. He was going to the one place that he was never allowed.

He knew how to get there because he had stowed away in the back one morning, angry that his father had told him no, yet again.

"Why can't I go?" Theo asked, holding back tears.

"You need to stay and help your grandmother," Abner would answer.

Theo's grandmother was a kind woman, and he loved her very much. She practically raised him. When she passed away, Theo was hit hard.

"Please!" he would beg.

"I said 'no.' Maybe next time," Abner would walk through the door and into the garage to grab his rod and reel. This happened for years, until Theo finally discovered the concept of rebellion. He decided to go along anyway. He snuck into the bed of the truck, and rode along in secret to his father's supposedly 'secret' place.

Theo was in his early teens at this point, and was sure his father was hiding something sinister. *Maybe he's a spy!* Theo would think, giving reason to his father's cold and distant demeanor. Imagination can be a steely armor.

Theo rode along, hidden in the bed of the trunk and following the signs as they turned onto a gravel road, and headed toward the river. From his position, leaning back and staying out of sight of the rear view mirror, he could see the bluffs passing by. The famous Villa Leila loomed over them. It seemed so much bigger when he was a kid. Abner made a quick right turn, and into a field. Theo never forgot that drive.

Theo took a sharp right onto an unmarked gravel road. The truck slid into the turn, launching the white rocks into the air as it leapt in gear. A dirty cloud of dust rose up behind. The white of the gravel looked so clean before it was scrambled into a cloud. It contrasted against the green grass, and brown husks of corn that lined the straight road.

He looked at the ocean of corn fields that disappeared in the distance. It was early September, and the corn was ready for its duty. It was harvest season. The heartland was in its golden years, soon to join the seasons past when the cold of the winter would finally kill it off, making room for the next generation.

Humanity is a funny thing. We're always trying to figure it out, when maybe the answer is simple. We learned how to farm. We learned how to raise a crop, and when to harvest, and how to keep it healthy. We bring it life and watch it grow, much like a member of our family. Yet, as we continue to bang away like rabbits on spring break, and more and more people join the journey, no one can hear the planet groaning under the weight. We learned how to modify crops through genetics. Farms don't need farmers anymore. Now, we need scientists to help us figure out how to enhance what the world already gave us just to help us live, when it may be scientists that one day kill us all.

Out of nowhere, a small red fox darted across the road. Theo hit the brakes and the truck slid through the loose gravel. He took a deep breath. It was so quick, but Theo could swear he could hear it laughing. "What a dick," Theo said under his breath as he continued on.

Pieces of Fall Creek began to appear on his left. A small trailer. A bulldozer in someone's front yard. What was once an old horse stable was now an auction yard. Old houses began to pop up. Ancient homes in the eyes of America. He saw an old woman sitting on a porch swing, staring right through him as he drove by. There was one right turn in the settlement, and then just as mysteriously as it appeared, Fall Creek disappeared into the rear view mirror. A mile later, Theo pulled over to the side of the road next to a very old, very small, wooden bridge. The bridge had been fenced off by the county years ago, due to safety reasons.

Theo walked the perimeter of the fence until he found the gate. It had been chained up loosely enough for him to squeeze under. He walked carefully across the decaying planks that crossed the creek, through the trees and into a small grove that surrounded a horseshoe shaped pool of water. At the far end of the fishing-hole stood a lonesome apricot tree, its roots bared by the eroding banks and sticking into the water. At the nearest end stood the outlet of the pool, where it connected to the creek that brought in water from the Mississippi River. Everything is connected.

The edges of the water were covered in floating moss. Willow trees surrounded the grove, and above the tree line in the close distance stood the bluffs where the beautiful Villa Leila kept watch over the waters. A pathway connected to a never used hiking trail that led up through the bluffs and into the villa's estate. It was a hell of a hike, but worth it for the view at the top. There was just enough sunlight peeking through the greenery that one could almost hear the soundtrack to Snow White. It was a place of peace.

Theo felt a tinge of guilt. He felt that he had the wrong reasons to come to a place like this. In his mind, he always hated this place, and now that he saw it he couldn't understand why. It was like going to church just to give God the finger.

He sat at the edge of the bank and didn't bother with the bait. He didn't feel like fishing anymore. He never really did to begin with. He just felt like sitting. He felt like drinking.

The surrounding trees kept the breeze out, and the water was still, except for the few small ripples from the comings and goings of bugs. The sounds of cicadas began in the distance. Theo saw something hanging from the branch of the lonesome apricot tree. It looked like a piece of yarn moving in the breeze. He stood up and walked toward it to investigate further. It was a pair of unmatched shoelaces. The bark had grown over the branch they were tied around, and only the ends were left dangling, as if they were part of the tree itself. *That's weird.*

He grabbed a hold of one of the laces and started to pull it out.

"Unhand that, you crumb!"

Theo dropped his hand instantly and turned around. "Hello??" he cried out. His heart began to pump a little bit faster and a little bit harder. There was no one around. He scanned the tree line and began walking away from the apricot tree slowly, his back to the water.

"Hello??" he yelled out again to no answer. There was a small splash behind him. Theo turned around quickly to see the ripples in the water. *Someone is throwing rocks.*

"If I'm trespassing, I'm sorry. I didn't think this was private land," he offered.

There was another splash. Theo caught a quick flicker of light reflecting off of the tail of a catfish as it snapped through the surface of the water, leaving behind a small ripple that would eventually disappear with time. He began to question whether he heard anything at all. *Maybe I'm finally losing it.*

He relaxed a bit and walked toward the tree again. "This is it," he laughed to himself, "Where I finally have my mental breakdown. It's been waiting in the wings for a while now."

He made his way back toward the apricot tree. A spray of water caught him on the cheek. He looked toward the water, and there, looking back at him, were two small, black eyes. The eyes were connected to a medium sized head of a fish breaking the water's surface. As Theo got closer, he could see that it was a catfish. Its whiskers were floating from the edges of its mouth. The dark brown skin shimmering in the light. Its beady little eyes were dark and unblinking.

"Well, hey there, little guy," Theo laughed, wiping the water from his cheek.

"Hey," the fish responded.

Theo stopped in his tracks. *Wait, what? No. Did that fish just answer me? Nope. I'm definitely losing it. My grasp on reality has been shattered. I blame the booze. Or the stress. Maybe too much smoke inhalation? Did I die in a fire? Am I dead? Have I been dead this whole time? That would make so much sense.*

They stared at each other for a moment, Theo afraid to blink, the catfish unable to.

"Okay, Theo. I think it's time to go home and take a nap," he muttered to himself as he turned and slowly walked away. "Maybe Heather has some pills I could have. Maybe some Xanax. That would be nice."

"Hell yeah, brotha. Hook it up! Hit me with some of those Xannies," the catfish spoke again. He had an enthusiasm in his voice that was impossible to fake. There was a strange joy in it.

The human mind, much like camels, can only carry so much weight. Eventually it all adds up, and then it only takes but one more straw to finally break its back. In this case, an annoyingly-optimistic, talking catfish was Theo's one-more-straw.

For a moment, he forgot about his injured leg and began to run. The pain shot through him like electricity. He hobbled back through the tree line and took the bridge with urgency. He landed in the driver's side of his father's old pick-up truck, started her up, and hit the gas before it was in gear. The gravel stirred

beneath the tires and he was gone in a cloud of dirty
white dust.

NINE

"911, what's your…"

"GAHHHSTAAAAVVV IS DEAD!!" Damian howled through the phone.

"Slow down, sir." The operator had a sense of confusion in her voice. "You say someone is dead?"

"Ya – yes… Gustav, my sweet angel… is dead!! GAAAAAHHH!" Damian cried out.

"Sir, I need you to calm down. Are you with Gustav at the moment?" The operator looked at the clock. Twenty minutes until her shift was over.

"NO, YOU NEED TO CALM DOWN, GODDAMMIT! A SEA MONSTER KILLED MY BABY! AHHHHHH!"

"Sir, I'm having trouble hearing you. Did you say a 'sea monster'?" The operator was thinking about finally putting in her two weeks and taking that trip to the Netherlands that she had been dreaming of.

"YOU HEARD ME, DAMN IT! A SEA MONSTER STABBED GUSTAV IN HIS PERFECT GOLDEN HEART! Oh lord….Ahhhh!" Damian was beside himself. He couldn't understand why this woman couldn't figure this out. An evil river monster killed his turtle. *Why is that so confusing?*

"Sir, we are nowhere near a sea," she answered. In her mind, she was smoking a joint on a pedal boat in the canals of Amsterdam.

"OH, SEMANTICS! TYPICAL! A RIVER MONSTER KILLED MY SWEET BOY, YOU EVIL WOMAN! WHY CAN'T YOU UNDERSTAND THIS?!"

"Sir, I'm sending over the police now. Are you alone?" she asked.

"…sniff… yes," Damian answered through tears.

"Okay, I have officers on the way to you. Please stay on the line."

"…sniff… okay."

TEN

Bernardino Perez sat on his porch swing drinking a decaf tea. He couldn't sleep. It had been a long life, and he was tired, but he just couldn't get to sleep. He watched the pink sunlight slowly peek up over the brown fields across the country road.

Detectives do not retire well. The thought echoed through his mind. He had given the Kenton P.D. forty-two years of his life. He had given retirement ten. He couldn't decide which was lasting longer. The average retired police officer dies within ten years of retirement. Dino took another sip.

"Having trouble sleeping?" His wife, Sarah stood at the door.

"These diuretics... I can't quit peeing." Dino took another sip of tea.

"Let's go to the city this weekend," she mentioned.

"Sure, that sounds fun." Dino smiled. He hated the city, but his wife loved it, and he loved her.

Sarah returned the smile and walked back into the bedroom. She was only a year into her retirement and was loving her new found freedom. She didn't make much from her time as an elementary teacher, but whatever was left she was bound and determined to spend.

Dino stood up and walked around the house and into the attached garage. He flipped on the lights over his work bench. He had spent most of his retirement lying to himself and others about how much he was enjoying it. He would fish. He would read. He would jog. Every once in a while, though, something would stir inside of him. He could still feel Detective Perez deep down. Dino was just a gray-haired old man with high blood pressure.

He flipped on the dusty police scanner that sat on the garage shelf. It clicked to life. There probably wasn't much going on this early in the morning, but he was feeling nosy. He had the same feeling that his younger self would have called a "hunch." He took a sip of his now cold tea. He missed coffee.

"This is Officer Bessling. I'm on scene. I'm approaching the residence," a voice through the scanner fuzzed.

Dino's ears perked up. *Oh boy, do we have a disturbance?*

"It was a turtle." There was a moment of silence on the scanner.

"Can you repeat that?" another voice fuzzed.

"Yeah, it was a pet turtle. Someone stabbed his pet turtle. Whack-job season started early this year," Officer Bessling answered.

Dino laughed to himself. *Kenton always delivers.* He reached up to turn the scanner off.

"He claims it was a monster from the river that did it," the officer repeated.

The retired detective paused. *No way. No way.* He turned up the volume.

"I'm sorry. I'm not hearing you correctly. Sounded like you said a river monster killed his turtle?" the voice on the scanner laughed.

"Copy that. A river monster. He insists we bring him in. He is pretty drunk," Officer Bessling said.

"What are you charging him with? Turtlecide?" Some laughter came through the fuzz.

"I need an APB for a 'Master Shredder.'" More laughter made its way through the fuzz.

Dino flipped the switch and turned the scanner off. He forgot his tea as he walked into the house. *No way. Can't be. Can it?*

ELEVEN

Huckleberry Gary knew the tunnels well. He patrolled them almost daily. He was scoffed at often, many times the butt of the joke. But, he knew that protecting the city from the reptiles was more important than his pride. The navy taught him that. Pride goeth before destruction.

Gary was on a mission, and so far so good. He had not yet failed in his task of letting the reptile overlords take this good city. It could be because he had actually never caught one, but that didn't matter. The shape-shifting reptiles were good at hiding. That was their strength. He knew this. He also knew that they were arrogant creatures. That was their weakness. A haughty spirit before a fall.

It was a chilly morning, but he was warm. He had on an old pair of coveralls that fit a little tighter than they used to. He carried a loaded Sig Sauer M9 nine-millimeter pistol on his right hip and a 6-inch Ontario MK stainless steel knife on his left; remnants of his days in the armed forces. On his back hung a pink crossbow that he bought from the Kenton pawn shop.

Huck, as usual, had a small hangover, but, as usual, it didn't slow him down one bit. He was learning a lot from his court ordered DUI classes, but the recidivism part hadn't quite stuck yet. Besides, he was carrying the weight of war on his shoulders. Not from the war in Afghanistan. Not from his time on board the

Boxer ARG. No, this was an unknown war, and he, the lone soldier. So yeah, he deserved a little downtime now and then. And what goes better with downtime than a bottle of Jameson Irish Whiskey?

The tunnels connected all throughout the bluffs that ran along the Mississippi River. There were many cave systems connected to a large man-made tunnel system that worked in tandem with the natural aquifer which was used by the brewery long ago. The brewery, which had been closed down for years, had survived prohibition by bottling water, sodas, and other types of non-alcoholic beverages during the day. At night they would use the tunnels to deliver kegs of beer and bottles of hooch to the river.

Some of the caves were bought and converted into storage facilities and warehouses by private companies. Some tunnels connected to the nearby streams and eventually led to the dam, just north of Kenton. Huck kept track of them all. He sometimes took a break from the dark underground and would patrol the islands on the river. Other times, he would check into the sewer systems.

Sure, he was laughed at by most of the town, but the Illuminati Reptilian Elite was no joking matter. He would explain to anyone who would listen that they had been around us for thousands of years with one goal: enslave the human race. The scariest part of it: they were winning. Huck couldn't help but feel that humanity was all but lost. The reptiles had shifted their blood drinking violence to a more sophisticated means of entrapment. They had given us what we thought we wanted. They were drowning the bees in their own honey.

How long can we survive in the age of the iPhone? How fragile are our hearts truly, as we watch one another thrive on Instagram, while secretly crumbling at home? We compare ourselves to a fantasy version of others, all the while longing for a connection that we will never get over 5G.

When success is measured in likes, and failure is measured in tweets, we can never reach Nirvana. Not when our only growth is found from buzzwords in Twitter posts written behind a thin veneer of enlightenment. What can a shaving commercial do for the plight of the disposable man? How can a meme lift the boots of rape culture off of our daughters' necks? If the answer is inward, then we are looking in the wrong place. Yes, the reptiles are winning.

There's no Facebook in Alpha Draconis. Huck pulled out a half empty flask from his back pocket and took a swig. A little Jameson always hit the spot on a hunt. He didn't care that no one believed him, and it didn't matter that he had no evidence. He was a soldier for humanity. He was doing this for us.

Huckleberry swore that he had seen one before, forty years ago, when he was just a little kid. It was dusk and he and his father had just loaded up their jon boat on the trailer and were getting ready to head home. They had been out on the river setting trout lines. It was early June, and the sun was setting later in the evening.

"Did you get the plug, Gary?" his father asked him as he finished winching the boat to the trailer.

"Doing it now," Gary called back. He whistled a hymn as he walked to the back of the boat to unplug it and drain the water.

There was a gurgling of bubbles and foam coming from the river bank a few feet behind him. Gary turned to see a tall human-like creature rise out of the water. It was black, with long arms and deep dark eyes. Gary screamed. His father ran to the back of the boat.

"What is it?!" he questioned.

Gary pointed at the water, but the creature was gone. His father grabbed him, and they got in the truck and sped off into the night.

"HOLY FUCKING SHIT!" Gary finally let out.

"Gary! Ephesians 5:4!" his father answered.

"I'm sorry, Pa."

"What was it that frightened you so much that you would let such corruptive talk come out of your mouth?" his father asked.

"It was a monster!" Huck said.

His father didn't believe his account, nor did anyone else after, but Gary knew in his heart that he saw something in the river that day.

It was when he came across the son of the Godhead, David Freaking Icke, dressed in turquoise and being interviewed on the television, that he finally knew what he had seen. The shape-shifting reptilian elite were on the planet all right. And they were right here in Kenton, Illinois. Huck knew that it was his responsibility to protect his town.

Huckleberry Gary shimmied in his coveralls, arranged his junk, and continued his patrol down the dimly lit tunnel.

TWELVE

Theo was standing in his late father's basement, unsure of where to even begin. There was too much stuff. He thought maybe he should start packing by category. He could start with the dusty lamps, or start with the collection of VCRs. Maybe move on to the box marked, "Christmas." Wait, no that was crossed out… "Kitchen." No, that had a line through it. There was a piece of tape on it that said "fragile." No, that had red marker scribbled over it. There it was… "X-mas."

Theo opened it up. It was full of old pictures. He picked one up and looked at it closely. It was a picture of him and his grandma. He was holding an Easter basket. He couldn't remember it, but here was the proof it happened. They looked happy.

Theo was up early today. He had trouble sleeping the night before. He blamed it on the fact that he had met a talking catfish, but it very well could have been the bottle of rum he used to try and forget about said fish. Either way, he was tired. And he couldn't get what happened at the grove out of his mind.

He carried the box up the stairs, through the kitchen, and out into the nearly cleared out garage.

"Hey, boner!" Theo heard a voice from the driveway. Heather was walking toward him holding a comically oversized cup of coffee with both hands. She was in an old camouflage t-shirt and tight black jeans.

"Hey, yourself," he smiled. He was happy to see her.

"How's packing?" she asked.

"It's an organizational nightmare," Theo responded, dropping the box to the garage floor.

"Well, I thought I would come over and check on you. Make sure you weren't drowning in despair," Heather said.

"Oh, I'm drowning alright. I'm thinking of just burning this whole place down and saving myself the headache."

"That would be dope." Heather took a sip from her coffee mug.

"What are you up to?" Theo asked.

"Well, I'm off today and tomorrow. Suzi will be done with work in a few hours. We are going to go get drinks later. You should join us!"

"Date night? I don't want to be a third wheel," Theo said.

"No, come on. It'll be fun. It will help get your mind off of things," Heather responded. She was right.

Theo laughed, "Okay. Sounds good to me."

"Peace, bitch," Heather turned around and moseyed back toward her house.

THIRTEEN

Dino Perez hated grocery shopping. His wife handed him a list this morning before giving him a "you can do it" pep talk. Before he knew it, he was out the door and at the local Hy-Vee. He was staring at the wall of yogurt before him, paying homage to the shrine of probiotics.

Cherry Cheesecake? He saw some cherry flavored. He saw some cheesecake flavored. He saw some strawberry cheesecake flavored. Where on earth was the cherry cheesecake? *Come on Dino, you solved a double homicide with nothing to go with but a bowling ball and a chicken bone. You can figure this one out.*

A middle aged lady was pushing a shopping cart by, talking on her cell phone. Her chopped hair cut stood proud and tall. "Did you hear about Sam??" she said, loud enough for everyone else to hear.

Dino moved aside as she easily found the yogurt she was looking for.

"Something killed his dog last night! I know, poor thing. He says it was some bigfoot-like creature. A 'swamp thing' he called it. Can you believe that? Their poor kid is hysterical." She moved away and continued down the aisle.

A swamp thing? Dino's ears perked up. *Another death of a beloved pet?* He followed her to the eggs. He waited for a few moments in hopes that she would hang up, but the woman just kept on talking.

"I'm sorry. I hate to interrupt..." Dino motioned toward the woman's phone.

"Hold on, Karen, some old Mexican needs me." She held her phone away, "Hola, como ayudo you?"

Dino couldn't figure out if that was racist or not, but he didn't care. Accidental racism was a common byproduct in Kenton. Most of the white folks meant no harm. In fact, they wore it as a badge of honor that they were so accepting and knowledgeable about the world around them. Their worldview was as opaque as a glass window in an old church. This lady couldn't wait to tell Karen about how she spoke Spanish with some old Mexican guy at the Hy-Vee. Her family would eat tacos for dinner. It didn't matter that Dino's heritage was Guatemalan.

"Uh... okay. Thanks. I'm sorry to interrupt your phone call. I couldn't help but overhear that your friend's dog was killed by some creature?" he asked.

"Mmhmm. It's mucho tragico." she said.

"Yes, it is...Very sad," Dino agreed. "These people...do they live near the river?"

"Yes! Yes they do!"

"And did this mucho tragic murder happen at night?"

"Yes it did! In the middle of the noche! How did you know?" She seemed surprised.

"Oh, I was just curious. Same thing happened to a guy I know. Must be a coyote or something. Thank you for your time!" Dino knew he owed her some Spanish. "Uh...gracias." Dino circled back to the yogurt section.

"TE NADA!" The woman called out to him. She was happy to help.

Dino grabbed a random yogurt and tossed it in his cart. This was no time for yogurt. He had questions that needed answers. *It's back!* He couldn't believe it. He sped toward the register and paid for the items. Dino had to visit the police station, but he needed an angle to avoid suspicion. He also needed to find this Damian, the River Rat fella and ask him about his dead turtle. *It started with pets last time. Someone in this town is going to be murdered soon.*

FOURTEEN

Mary Ann had very little patience. She did not learn this from her mother, who seemingly had an endless supply. It takes infinite patience to raise an impatient child.

It was 9:30 p.m. Mary Ann had just finished up her shift at the gas station and was now standing in her mother's living room with the front door open. She wore a similar expression on her face to those who are waiting to deboard an airplane.

Mary Ann worked at the gas station across the bridge on the Missouri side of the river, where gas prices were often fifteen to twenty cents lower per gallon than the greedy Illinois prices. Residents of Kenton would drive for miles to cross the bridge and fill the tank. Mary Ann couldn't help but wonder if some of them were actually saving money at all, burning up the gas to get there. She surmised that human nature cares about numbers, but not about math.

"LET'S GOOO?" she questioned the sky, hoping to be answered by both her mother and the Lord above.

An elderly woman of eighty-five years hobbled through the door and into the living room. She wore an old blue jacket, over an even older sweatshirt with two adorable rabbits embroidered into the chest. There was a plastic rain bonnet, dry from the clear skies, covering freshly curled hair that looked like it had been painted a shade of light brown by hand, and faded by time. A hint of white roots were peeking up from the skull as a subtle reminder that you can run, but you can't hide.

Love lives inside of us in strange ways. Sometimes it's easy to forget it when you've known someone for your entire existence. Mary Ann loved her mother, but she often kept that love in her pockets, and instead wore her frustrations on her sleeve.

"Good Lord, you are slower than molasses," she said as she shut the door quickly.

"Oh, quiet you," her mother let out as she made her way into the kitchen. It was almost bedtime, and she needed her evening tea. She set the kettle on the burner and went down the hall to change her clothes.

The two of them had just returned from BINGO night. Every Thursday, after Mary Ann would finish her shift, she would go to the Knights of Columbus hall and pick up her mother. It could be grating to the nerves, but was a better option than letting her mother drive herself. It was for the good of humanity.

Mary Ann turned on the small TV in the living room and set the station to seventeen, the channel that showed her mother's "stories." She did this at night when she would drop her off to avoid a phone call the next day, when her mother couldn't figure out how to change the channel.

The kettle whistle began to blow. It was loud and obnoxious and caught Mary Ann off guard, giving her a startle.

"Ma! Your tea!" Mary Ann hollered into the hallway. There was no answer. The whistle kept blowing. The train was leaving the station. Mary Ann stood up and walked into the kitchen. "Your tea is ready! Hello?" Still no answer.

She turned the burner off and placed the kettle on one of the others.

"Mom?" A brief moment of worry blew through Mary Ann.

Her mother appeared like a spectre from the dark hallway in a nightgown and glasses.

"I heard you! I'm not deaf!" She made her way past her daughter and fumbled through the cabinets before finding her tea. She placed a packet in the water and let it steep.

"Okay, well I'm going to go home now. Enjoy your tea. I will be back Saturday morning to pick you up for your eye appointment. Please be ready by ten. Please. I'm begging you. With all the strength I have within me. Ten o'clock - a.m. - In the morning."

Her mother stirred her tea, looking out the window.

"MA!" Mary Ann said.

"Hmmm?" her mother turned around, giving her daughter her full attention.

"I said I'll be here on Saturday MORNING at TEN O'CLOCK. Can you please be ready?"

"Yes, yes. I heard you. I'm not deaf!" She took a sip of her tea.

Mary Ann said goodbye and let herself out of the house. She walked toward the short driveway and clicked the button on her keys to unlock the car door. It was a cool, clear night, and the moon seemed bigger than normal in the sky. Its light was bright enough that the street lights seemed futile.

She heard something move through the fallen leaves behind her. She turned around quickly, but saw nothing. *Probably a raccoon or a stray cat or something,* she thought. She got into the driver's seat of her car. Something didn't feel right. She couldn't place the sense of dread.

The car took a few tries to start up. She backed out and headed toward her home, a half a mile away. Her apartment building was dark when she pulled into her usual parking spot. Everyone was either sleeping or at the bar.

Mary Ann's apartment was on the third floor, but she always took the stairs. This way she could justify the fact that she didn't have to exercise. She lived an active lifestyle. She stopped at the second floor. That feeling of dread came over her again. Something was not right. She turned around and decided to head back to her mother's.

******

Ma was almost asleep. She was lying on her back in bed. The house was quiet until the sound of glass crashing. Ma didn't hear it, even though she was not deaf. A dark figure made its way into the bedroom and stood over the half-asleep old woman. The moonlight shone through the window and reflected off of the mossy surface of the creature.

"Mary Ann? What are you doing back here?" her mother asked.

The creature raised its hand over her, its long fingers fused in a grip with the old rusted dagger.

"Wait, wait, wait…" the old woman said, ignoring the danger above her, "Let me get my glasses on. Is something wrong, dear?"

The monster froze, waiting on the woman to find her glasses. It seemed confused. It had never been told to wait before. It mostly just heard screaming and begging.

Ma felt around the nightstand. "Now where are my glasses..?" she mentioned to herself. Her hand found a glass cup where she kept her dentures. "No, no, no. Not these."

The creature stood there ready to strike.

"Don't just stand there, now. Help me find my glasses."

The monster lowered his arm. He looked around the dresser. No glasses. Mary Ann turned on the lamp next to the bedside table. The monster was taken aback. He hated the light.

"Maybe they are in the kitchen," Ma said.

At that moment, they heard the front door open.

"Ma? You awake," Mary Ann called into the house. She began to walk toward the bedroom.

The monster heard this and immediately went back to action. He grabbed the confused old woman by the arm and laid her back in bed. He took aim with the dagger and quickly stabbed her through the heart. Mary Ann's mother took a large breath, and exhaled hard, breathing the life right out of herself.

Mary Ann walked into the bedroom and saw the river creature over her mother. The creature was six feet tall. He was shiny and black and covered with moss and ooze. Swampy. He smelled like mud. The light blue eyes looked human. There was a mouth and a nose, but they seemed to have no purpose. The blade was fused to his hand with moss and vines. The creature pulled the knife from her mother's chest, its rusted blade now covered in blood. Mary Ann was frozen in terror.

The creature slammed past her, knocking Mary Ann to the ground. It moved quickly, but unsteadily, like a newborn deer just learning how to walk. The creature made its way out the same way it came in, through a broken glass door that opened to the small backyard. A jagged shard of glass grabbed hold and ripped a tattered piece of cloth from the creature's old, waterlogged shirt.

Mary Ann stood up, collected her panicked breathing, and screamed.

FIFTEEN

One of the four speakers in the Cherry Street Tavern had been blown out for years. The low bass tones were buzzing through it, but no one in the packed bar seemed to care. It was a Friday night, and Kenton was up late. Damian, the River Rat sat on his usual stool with his usual drink, but was unusually drunk. He was telling his story to anyone who would listen.

"I'm telling you it was some sorta demon! I looked it right in the eyes. It was pure evil!" he slurred.

"Wow," a random patron said with feigned empathy as they looked for any other open spots to sit, "That's crazy."

The bar was lined up with camouflage hats and work boots. There was laughter and big voices all around. In the corner of the bar, Huckleberry Gary was shooting pool with a guy in an army jacket. He would hang with the local veterans and talk with them about their PTSD. He found that helping others with their trauma helped him with his own.

Theo walked in through the back door and bumped into an older man leaning against the jukebox, waking him up from a drunken slumber. He excused himself and let the man get back to sleep. He found Heather and Suzi at a table near one of the few windows.

"Theo!" Suzi jumped up and gave him a big hug. Heather poured him a beer from their pitcher.

"Sorry I'm late. I had to drop Saylor off with her mom. She met me halfway from the city. I'm going to get her back here next weekend."

"How is the Queen of Badgers?" Heather asked.

"Heather! Oh my god!" Suzi punched her in the arm.

"What? She looks like a badger." Heather defended herself.

"Oh my. She doesn't look like a badger, Theo." Suzi had always been the peacemaker.

"Actually, today I was thinking she kind of had a 'wolverine' thing going on," Theo said. They laughed as they lifted their glasses and made a toast.

******

Huckleberry Gary approached the bar to order another round of drinks. He stood next to Damian and waited for the bartender. He was no longer armed to the teeth. Instead he was in his casual wear: jeans and a black t-shirt.

"Another round, Huck?" Sheila, the bartender, asked. Huck nodded. Damian turned his body toward him and held up his drink.

"To Gustav," Damian said.

"I don't have anything to cheers ya with, man." Huck held up an empty bottle.

"Oh… Well we can try again," Damian put his beer back down and lowered his head.

"Who is Gustav?" Huck asked.

"Only the best friend a man could ask for! He was killed a few nights ago. Murdered by a devil!"

"No shit? I'm sorry to hear that. He was murdered?" Huck asked.

"You'll just laugh at me like the rest of these mouth breathers. I'm not crazy. I know what I saw!" Damian put his head down.

The bartender set down the round in front of Huck. He smiled politely. "You'd be surprised. I've heard a lot of things. Try me." Huck offered.

Damian told him the story of the river monster. How it stood tall as a man and had dark hollow eyes and had a long blade. Moss hung from its shoulders and he smelled like wet clay. He told him about how it threw him aside and flipped Gustav over on his shell and stabbed him through the heart. When Damian tried to fight back, it just pushed him away like he was nothing and went back into the river.

"So this creature just killed your turtle and left?" Huck questioned.

"He took the only thing I loved from me." Huckleberry Gary took this information in. He had trouble hiding his smile.

"To Gustav," Huck raised his beer. Damian clinked his bottle and nodded. Huck walked back to his crew. *Illuminati.* He believed the man. Or maybe he just wanted to believe him. Either way, he had a new area to recon in the morning.

******

A slow blues song came on over the jukebox. An older couple began to dance. A line formed outside the one stall bathroom. Kenton was slipping into full gear.

"I saw something kind of weird yesterday," Theo said. He was loosened up and letting the beer do the talking for him.

"What's that?" Suzi asked.

"Well… I went fishing," Theo wasn't sure how to explain it, "and I met a fish."

"You caught a fish?" Heather laughed. "Isn't that the goal? Great story, Theo."

"No, I MET a fish," he corrected.

"You met a fish?" Heather asked. It didn't make sense.

"Yeah, I could have sworn this fish spoke to me," Theo stared at the wall.

"What did it say, Theo?" Suzi asked.

Theo felt stupid. He couldn't believe the words that came out of his mouth. *I met a fish? Come on.*

"Forget it. I know it didn't happen. It was just very, very strange," he said.

"No! What did it say? You can't say you met a talking fish and then not give the details!" Heather said.

"It said it wanted some Xanax," Theo couldn't help but laugh at his own insanity.

"It wants some Xanax?" Heather asked.

"Yeah…. This catfish…. Well, it wants some Xanax," Theo said. They all laughed at the absurdity of it.

"Theo, honey, I think maybe that was your subconscious saying that you want some Xanax," Heather said as she grabbed Suzi by the waist, "Come on, woman. Let's go smoke a joint and make out by the dumpsters. We will let Dr. Doolittle get the next pitcher." They stood up giggling and in love.

Theo grabbed his wallet from his coat and went to the bar. He stood waiting for the bartender when he was bumped by a woman.

"Oh gosh, excuse me!" She had on comically oversized sunglasses and couldn't stop laughing. There was a small tattoo of a maple leaf on her right arm that matched the colors of her auburn hair. Something about her made Theo nervous, and he had trouble finding words.

"Is your future pretty bright?" *Come on Theo, you idiot.*

"What?" She laughed.

"I mean… 'cause of you have to wear shades," Theo stumbled.

"Oh… Yep!" She smiled and grabbed her drink and joined her friends. They all had the same giant sunglasses on and were celebrating a bachelorette party. The soon-to-be-bride was very drunk and telling one of her friends how beautiful she was and how much she loved her.

Theo went back to the table and sat alone. *Maybe I should try dating again.* It had been two years since his split with his ex-wife. When that happened, he just dug into his work at the fire department. He loved that job. He couldn't wait to get back to it. Theo moved his injured knee slowly. He knew he needed surgery, but couldn't seem to find time in the midst of all of his new found free time. It's funny how slippery time can be.

Suzi came back to the table first. She sat down and looked at Theo.

"Is that Huckleberry Gary?" Theo asked as he pointed toward Gary. He was leaning over the pool table breaking up a game of Eight Ball.

"Yes, it is," Suzi answered. "He's still... an interesting fella."

"Yeah, I remember," Theo said. "He was a few years older than me, but I remember him being kind of... I don't know the word for it."

"Intense?" Suzi asked.

"Dumb," Theo answered.

"That's not nice! He's always been sweet to me," Suzi said in his defense.

"I remember for Halloween one year he dressed as a piñata," Theo said. "Everyone beat the crap out of him."

"Okay, that may not have been the smartest idea for a costume," Suzi said. The two of them laughed.

Heather rejoined the table with shots of whiskey. Theo and Suzi groaned in unison.

"Theo, I've been thinking about your new fish friend. I think that maybe what you need is some good old fashioned sleep. Here," She smiled and pushed one of the shot glasses toward him. "This will help," she said.

SIXTEEN

It was morning. Dino walked into the Kenton Detective Unit carrying a plate of freshly baked brownies. The smell was a welcome contrast to the stale coffee flavored air.

There was a grand total of six detectives on the Kenton P.D., and they could usually be found playing online poker at their desks. The occasional gas station robbery or car theft kept them busy enough to justify the department's budget, but not so much that they didn't enjoy a little easy-earned R&R. This morning, however, the desks were empty.

Not much had changed in Dino's ten years away. The sunrise still shined through the line of windows on the far wall like he remembered. The quiet hum of fluorescent lights buzzed in the panel ceiling. On one end of the room stood a row of cabinets and an empty coffee pot, stained from the years of half-caf coffee. On the opposite end of the room was an open door that led to the captain's office.

"Dino, nice to see you. To what do I owe this surprise?" Captain Ross stood behind him.

"Captain!" Dino turned to face him and shook his hand. "Just thought I'd pop in and see how things are going. Sarah made some brownies, and I have no self-control, so I thought I'd dump them off here."

"Well, thank you, Dino. So, retirement still treating you well?" The captain asked.

"I love it," Dino said as he looked around. "Where's the crew?"

Captain Ross had come into the detective's unit after Dino had already established himself as a respected member of the squad. He looked up to Dino for years, and learned a lot from the seasoned veteran. The captain was diligent and worked hard, climbing the ranks with ease. He was promoted to captain the year Dino retired.

"They're on assignment. It's been a busy couple of days."

"Don't tell me Kenton has another serial streaker," Dino laughed.

"No, it's a little more serious than that... gas station robbery," the captain said.

"Nothing like a good old fashioned smash and grab." Dino looked around the room.

"So how are things?" Captain Ross led him into his office and took a seat behind his desk. "How is Sarah?" he asked.

Dino placed the plate on the desk and sat down across from him. "Sarah is great. Things are good. We are talking about going to the city this weekend," he said.

"That's good to hear. Please tell her I send my love."

"Will do," Dino said.

"So what can I do for ya? What's up?" Captain Ross asked.

"Well... This is kind of embarrassing, but I've been working on a memoir. And, well, I'd love to get a few copies of some of my old case files, just so I make sure I get it right. Don't want to slander anyone..."

"Libel," the captain corrected.

"Ahh, right. Maybe you could edit it for me?" Dino laughed.

"Oh I don't know if you want that!" The captain smiled. "So a memoir, huh? That sounds interesting. Is this for a publishing thing or..?"

"No, no. Nothing like that. I just thought it would be nice. Figured I should write it now, while I still have my memories. Something to leave the kids for when I'm gone."

"That's a great idea. Hell, I'd love to read it myself," Captain Ross said.

"Sure, I'll get you a copy; I'll just omit your rookie years!" They shared a laugh.

"So Dino…" Captain Ross leaned forward. His eyebrows furrowed. "Why are you lying to me?" he asked.

"I'm sorry?" Dino said.

"Look, I know that you're a straight shooter. I like to think of myself as a straight shooter, too. So why don't we get to the point and shoot straight here? Sarah didn't make those brownies."

"What do you mean?" Dino said.

"These brownies have a curved edge, which leads me to believe that these brownies were baked in a round pan," Captain Ross said.

"What does that have to do with anything?"

"Dino, the average baking enthusiast uses an eight-inch square pan, greased. The greased bottom is essential in preventing the brownies from sticking, thus reinforcing their structural integrity. These brownies are also crumbling on the edges, and the tops are a little darker than normal. This also tells me that whoever did bake these brownies followed the directions on the box to perfection, leaving them in a pre-baked oven for twenty-one minutes... the average between twenty and twenty-two minutes... at three-hundred-fifty degrees," Captain Ross continued. "This is what most people would do, however, we both know that Sarah is well above average when it comes to baking delicious treats, and she knows better than most, that in order to maintain that ooey-gooey chocolate brownie delectability, one must remove the brownies from the oven within five to ten minutes *before* they are done. So, Dino, what all of this tells me is that Sarah, the baking enthusiast, did not make these sub-par brownies. No, someone else made these brownies, and that someone else is most likely... you. So I will repeat my question. Why are you lying to me?"

Dino sat in his chair and studied the captain. "Well Cap, I suppose I could ask you the same thing," he said.

"Oh?" Captain Ross leaned back.

"When I arrived this morning, I thought it was interesting how clean the floors were. Usually at this point in time, the floor would have been well traversed and scuffed from the usual traffic. Maybe a coffee spot here and there... crumbs from a muffin... but no... the floors are spotless. Sure, office protocol dictates the need for a clean work space, but doesn't the cleaning crew usually come in and tidy up overnight? So why is that wet floor sign and mop bucket still standing in the back corner? There must have been a mess this morning. Could have been anything, I suppose. Maybe Detective Shelly dropped an ice cream cone... innocent enough. It wasn't until I noticed your shoes that I realized."

"My shoes are spotless," Captain Ross said.

"No, not those shoes, Captain... THOSE shoes!" Dino pointed to a pair of dirty boots underneath the coat hanger near the office door. Dino stood from his chair and approached the shoes.

"Tactical Pursuit Oxford Five-Elevens if I'm not mistaken... a great choice for an officer in the field... lightweight, comfortable, and excellent traction. However, these particular boots seem to be covered in something. Mud perhaps?"

Dino crouched down and inspected the dirty boots. He placed a finger in the dried mud and put it to his mouth.

"Hmmm, just as I suspected. Silty clay. This is Gorham silty clay loam... not to be confused with Beaucoup soils, which obviously have a higher amount of clay in the subsoil..."

"Obviously," Captain Ross agreed.

"Now, Gorham silty clay loam is found in low lying areas as well as the flood plains. Areas close to the water. This tells me that you were recently down by the river. And if memory serves, I don't recall any gas stations down by the river?" Dino said.

"Does this have a point?" Captain Ross was visibly annoyed.

"Yes, Craig, it does. From my knowledge, captains don't usually go into the field, and if they do it's rarely for something as small fry as a gas station robbery? So tell me, Captain Ross, why were you working a gas station robbery down by the river where there aren't even any gas stations to be robbed?" Dino asked.

The two sat silently for a moment.

"I guess we're both not being completely honest with each other, hmm?" the captain offered.

"I suppose not," Dino grabbed a brownie and took a bite. They weren't as good as his wife's.

"You thought those brownies would make a good cover for your excuse to come by, and the 'memoirs' a good cover to ask for access to some old case files," Captain Ross said.

"And you didn't want to tell me about the dead pets and the river monster sightings," Dino added.

"I'm afraid it's more than just some dead pets."

"Oh?" Dino leaned in.

"We have a body. An elderly woman was murdered in her bed last night. Her daughter witnessed someone running out the back door. I've got officers with her there now."

"Someone?"

"Dino…"

"You were down by the river chasing a *someone*?" Dino said.

"Chasing a lead," Captain Ross corrected.

"I need those files, Craig."

"Dino…"

"Come on, man. This thing, whatever it is, if it's back and is killing people again, then I'm your best chance at finding it!" Dino said.

"Dino, the last thing I need is some seventy-something-year-old retired detective getting involved and interfering with a murder investigation. Especially someone who is convinced that the culprit is some damned 'river monster.' You know I respect you. Come on. Why not just go home and enjoy retirement? Take Sarah to the city like you were saying," Captain Ross said. Dino sat in frustration.

"Well, I guess I could go talk to someone at the paper. I'm sure they can dig up some old articles. I remember the paper really loved writing about the mysterious 'Creature from the Mississippi,'" he said.

"A thinly veiled threat? Really?" The phone beeped. Captain Ross answered. "Yeah?"

There was a murmur on the other line. Dino tried to listen in, but he didn't need to. The captain's face was telling enough.

"Okay. Tell Shelly that I'll be down there soon," he hung up.

"What is it?" Dino asked.
The captain stood up and put his muddy shoes back on. He grabbed his coat off of the rack. "Another body," he said.

"I'm coming with you," Dino said.

"No… just give me a second," Captain Ross began rubbing his temples. "Look, just… you can take pictures or scans or whatever, but the original files do not leave this building."

"Of course," Dino said.

"And please do not go to the papers. We will be overrun with phone calls, and I do not want people getting hurt because a bunch of random hillbillies are out hunting for Bigfoot," the captain pleaded.

"You got it. Thank you, Captain," Dino said.

Captain Ross grabbed a brownie on his way out.

SEVENTEEN

Theo woke up face down on the couch. The hangover was present and immediate. His face hurt, and dread was pulsing through his entire existence. *I need a pizza. A pizza will help fight this incurable existential crisis.* Standing up was going to be tough, but he powered through it, walked into the kitchen and drank straight from the faucet. The cold water poured into him like soft light through an opened curtain.

He could only manage to think of two things. First was, obviously, the pizza. Second was the woman with the maple leaf tattoo. It was her laugh. Theo knew better than to have a crush, though. A crush? That's for kids with open hearts. After a tough divorce, and losing his best friend to a fire, Theo decided it best to keep his heart closed. Life is hard on the heart. It's had a target on its back from the onset of time, the vulnerable, vulnerable heart.

Theo brushed his teeth and shook the hangover off with a quick shower. He put on some clean clothes, grabbed the keys, and walked out the front door to find his truck missing.

"Oh hell," he said, remembering a drunkenly wise decision to walk rather than drive last night.

His truck was still parked at the Cherry Street Tavern, two miles away. The only cab service in Kenton was run by a known arsonist named Paul, who drove an old Ford Windstar. Being the career firefighter that he was, Theo preferred not to hire the services of a fire bug, so he began walking.

******

Huckleberry Gary had just finished up his morning patrol and was grabbing a cup of coffee from the downtown café. He noticed Theo walking by and ran across the street to catch up with him.

"Theodore Beckett!" Gary said as he approached.

"Hi Gary," Theo responded.

"I saw you at the bar last night and meant to say hello, but it got a little blurry."

"Yes, it did." Theo kept walking.

Gary kept pace, pulled out a flask and offered it to Theo. "Hair of the dog?" he asked.

"No, thank you," Theo said.

Gary shrugged and added a little to his coffee. "Gotta keep the wolf off my back, man," He took a long, slow sip. "It's been a long time, man. How long you in town?"

Theo remembered Gary from high school. He remembered that Gary would often wear Stone Cold Steve Austin t-shirts and was one of the last to figure out how to shave the pencil mustache that he had sported since twelve years old. He was always an outsider looking in. Theo and his friends were always nice to Gary, but they never let him into their circle. Kids can be mean even when they aren't trying to be.

"Undecided. I have some things to take care of, and I'm currently on leave from the fire department. No real rush to get back, I suppose. Just depends on how long I can take being back."

"Big Chicago fire fighter, huh?" Huck said.

"Huge." They walked in silence. Theo's leg began to ache. "So, what's the crossbow for?" Theo asked.

"Oh, this?" Huck pulled the bow from his back and held it with pride, "Pretty sweet, huh? Well, between you and me, there's some goofy business going on in this town. I'm keeping an eye on things." He took a swig of his whiskey flavored coffee. "Things aren't what they seem. I got a gut feeling about it. You know anything about the illuminati?"

Oh, good lord. "No I don't, really," Theo lied. He knew as much as the average person knew, but that's a can of worms he did not want to open.

"Well, keep your eyes open for anything out of the ordinary. You came back to town at a strange time, Theo," Huck said.

"Will do, Gare-Bear."

Gary gave him a pat on the back and returned back up the street. He had to get ready for his DUI class before his usual afternoon patrol.

Theo thought, *Poor guy was never quite right, but who am I to judge? I talk to fish.* That reminded him. He was in such a scramble to get out of the grove that he left the fishing pole and tackle box behind. He would go grab it after lunch. He didn't mind the idea of clearing his mind of all that fish nonsense either.

******

Dino set a thick folder down on the workbench in his garage. Although Captain Ross had been explicit in that he could only take scans of the case files, Dino didn't care. *What's he going to do? Fire me?* He opened the folder and began to spread the pages across the sawdust covered bench. The morning was slowly turning to afternoon, and the light had shifted from the window, revealing the shadows that had been waiting all morning for their turn. Dino plugged in an old painter's light and dedicated it to the pile of documents.

It was 1985 when the monster first attacked, although the files told things differently than Dino remembered. He was eighteen years into a good career with the Kenton Police Department, and in his tenth year as a detective. He was well respected by his colleagues then. He thought that eventually he would be a captain.

It was young love. The kid was sixteen years old. He was stabbed once through the heart with a long blade. His girlfriend was beside herself. They had been parked out by the riverfront late that night, and she swore it was some creature that had done it. Not all the evidence pointed to her, but there was enough to convict.

Two months later, another victim was found. This time it was a murder-suicide. The bodies were found on one of the islands, now known to the locals as "Dead Men Island." Two men were found lying next to each other, dead. One of them had a similar stab wound through the heart, the other died of a self-inflicted gunshot wound from a small handgun. What was interesting about this case was that there were bullet holes found in a few of the surrounding trees. It was as if the man was shooting at something before taking his own life.

Winter came, and the killings stopped. Dino fell back into the comfort of the small-time crimes. He busted up the occasional trailer park robbery. He stopped a small drug ring. He enjoyed his holidays. Life was back to normal.

The next spring the murders began again, but now they were increasing in frequency. Kenton had a serial killer it seemed, and Dino Perez felt the crushing pressure to find them. Even more confusing, the victims seemed to have very little in common. There were old people, young people, pets; there was even an old man's bible that had been torn to shreds. They all seemed to say the same thing, though. It was a dark creature that smelled like clay and was covered in moss. It was a devil, come from the river.

Dino scanned the pages. He opened up the final report, and remembered it well. This was the only time he had a suspect. However, he could never find enough evidence to make an arrest. He knew in his gut, though, that this man was involved somehow. The last victim was a woman, thirty years old. She was eight months pregnant. She and her husband were out walking by the Riverside Park one evening. Every one of the victims was stabbed through the heart, clean. It was almost surgical. However, this time it was through the stomach. The doctors managed to save the baby, but the woman didn't survive. Could this have been a copycat that had gotten a little sloppy? The husband never mentioned a monster. In fact, he didn't say much at all.

He only claimed that it was done by a man with a hood on.

The killings stopped after this. No more river monsters. The newspapers eventually found other things to talk about, like the yearly chicken wing contest at the fairgrounds, or even worse, the communists that were all around us, hidden in plain sight.

Dino set the report down. It was thirty years ago. This new killing was most likely someone obsessed over the story of the monster, and that's why these murders have begun again.

He could never put a killer to that old case, and it eventually went cold. He knew he had missed something, and that something haunted him for years. He kept the feelings in the deep place where we keep our failures and mistakes and use fate and circumstance as a reason for them. The husband knew more than he let on, and Dino didn't push him hard enough back then. He didn't need to look back at the papers for the name. Dino never forgot it. It was Abner Beckett. He decided to pay him a visit.

EJGHTEEN

The clear sky and cool air helped ease Theo's mind as he made his way on the gravel back toward his father's secret fishing hole. A large green combine rolled slowly in the distance, harvesting the brown corn. The farmers would repeat their mantra. Make your hay while the sun is shining. A beautiful day in the heartland.

He pulled over and parked next to the old foot bridge. He had yet to eat his pizza and find that saving grace he needed, but decided to get some errands out of the way first. Checking this one off was first on his list. He cut through the narrow tree line and stepped into the small grove. The apricot tree stood before him, the shoelaces swaying in the indiscernible breeze. The water was a perfect mirror reflecting only blue from the cloudless sky. The sound of frogs buzzed in the distance. A man could take one hell of a nap.

Theo hurried toward the fishing gear that he had forgotten. He wanted to be in and out quickly, as one walks up the stairs from the basement after they turn the lights off. *Eat my dust demons!* He felt silly about hiding his presence from a fish, so he stopped to take a good look at the pond. A bug landed on the water's surface, breaking up the smooth with one slow ripple. Curiosity got the better of him. He went back to the gravel road and picked up some rocks.

Tossing rocks in the water is one of the defining aspects of what it is to be human. No matter where you are from, whether you are rich or poor, young or old, everyone loves to throw rocks into the water. It's part of our biological imperative.

Theo gave in to the intrinsic nature of humanity and started tossing. He threw them one at a time, and then waited for any reaction. Nothing. He continued, one at a time. Still nothing. Then, just as every fireworks display needs a grand finale, and every opera needs an aria, every rock throwing session needs an apex of its own. Theo took a handful of rocks and tossed them all at once, peppering the water with a number of little impacts.

"WHAT THE SHIT IS GOING ON UP HERE?!" the catfish yelled through gurgles as he burst through the surface, looking around incredulously. Theo plopped down at the edge of the water, his mouth agape. The fish looked at him.

"You!" he said, "What the hell, man?"

Theo searched for words but came up short. Nothing could compute. He just sat there and stared back.

"Do you have any idea what that's like?" the fish said before diving back down in the water.

"Uh… I'm sorry," Theo spit out, looking around for the fish.

The catfish popped back up and spit one of the rocks back at Theo. He blocked it with his arm.

"Dude, look at the size of those rocks compared to me? It was like fucking Pompeii down here, man!" the angry fish continued.

"Pompeii…" Theo repeated. His mouth wasn't working with him.

"Yeah, they had, like, a terrible eruption a long time ago. Mount Vesuvius..," the catfish said.

"Yeah, no… I know. I mean… You… Are you talking?" Theo asked.

"Stratovolcano… Crazy shit, man. Those poor Italians."

"Yeah, poor Italians…wait… wait a second, what the hell is going on here? Am I crazy?"

The catfish swam toward the bank and looked up at Theo. His whiskers floated next to his head. Dark eyes reflected the sky. "What are you doing here? How did you find this place?" the catfish spoke.

"I left my fishing pole here, and I wanted to come back and get it," Theo said. He wasn't sure how else to explain his presence.

"Yeah, I remember. Did you bring me any Xanax?" the catfish asked.

"Xanax? No…"

"Well thanks for nothing..," The catfish flipped over and started floating on its back. He started humming the melody to "Mr. Jones" by the Counting Crows. Theo sat there watching. He couldn't believe this.

The fish popped back up and looked at Theo. "Do you like the Counting Crows?" he asked.

"No, not really," Theo answered.

"WHAT?!"

"I think they are whiny and pompous," Theo explained.

"Whiny and pompous? Maybe you are crazy," the catfish said.

"It's like, we get it, man. You had a hard breakup. We don't need four albums about it."

"Unbelievable... So you wouldn't be upset if Jennifer Aniston broke up with you?"

"That's actually a great point," Theo said.

"I love Counting Crows, man," The fish began floating around again. "They sing about love."

"Love? All they sing about is pain and suffering and loneliness," Theo said as he sat down on the edge of the water.

"Sounds like love to me. It's beautiful, man," the catfish said,

"Oh, you know a lot about love, huh?"

"I know everything about love. That's why I'm here."

"Sure... Well, I'd love to learn all the secrets someday." Theo said. He chortled at how silly all of this was.

"What's your name?" the catfish asked.

"Theo. Do fish have names? Do you have a name?" Theo asked.

The catfish stopped swimming and looked back at him. If he had eyebrows they would have most certainly been furrowed in an intense and thoughtful way, but since he didn't, he just kind of stared.

"Theo?" he said, "You're Abner's kid?"

Theo stood up. This kept getting weirder. "How the hell do you know my dad?" he asked.

"You're Abner's kid?! Oh. My. Gosh! Your dad... he's my best and oldest friend!" the catfish said. He slapped his tail onto the surface of the water with a *hot damn* attitude.

"Then you were the only one he had," Theo said.

"What? I haven't seen him in a while. Where the hell is he? You need to bring him back here! He'll bring me some Xanax," the catfish said.

"Well, I'm sorry to have to tell you this. He died... a few days ago. Pancreas. It didn't take long."

"Abner's dead?" the fish asked.

"Yeah. I'm just in town for the arrangements. Cleaning out the house. That kind of stuff."

"Abner's dead..." he repeated to himself.

"Sorry," Theo offered.

The catfish floated in silence for a moment. Theo couldn't help but feel for the little guy. He never knew his father to have any friends, and certainly not a talking fish in a secret grove. What else was he hiding?

"Theo, listen...," the fish began. "There's bad magic in this river. I have to go and check on something. I'm sorry. Come back tomorrow." With that, the catfish dove under the surface. His tail made a tiny splash as he disappeared into the dark waters.

Theo ran closer to the pond. "Wait, wait, wait! I have about a hundred questions! Firstly, who the hell are you?!" Theo yelled into the water to no answer. *There's bad magic in this river.* The thought stayed with him.

NINETEEN

It was dark out when it happened," the instructor said as he stood up from the table abruptly. He walked with an air of importance toward the whiteboard and grabbed a dry erase marker. He began to draw a diagram of a highway.

Oh my God, this was it! Huckleberry Gary had been waiting for this moment. It had been eight weeks of drug and alcohol awareness classes that he was required to attend, thanks to a recent DUI; and for those eight weeks he and his six other classmates had been sharing their stories, silently judging each other, yet feigning support. His instructor, however, had yet to share his, and Huckleberry Gary had a gut feeling that something terrible had happened. Why else become an instructor in a class like this, if not to find some sort of redemption? The mystery, it seemed, was finally going to be solved.

"Are you guys familiar with the exit just outside of Marblehead, on I-72?" the instructor asked the small class. Huckleberry Gary's ears perked up. *Oh man! Did he kill someone?! I bet he killed someone! Wait, why am I excited about that? I'm not excited. I mean, I'm excited for the story, but not the terrible deaths. Am I a shitty person? Those poor people... People? Am I hoping he killed more than one person? No! No, of course not. That would be awful.*

"It was around Christmas time, and the roads were very icy," he continued. "There wasn't much traffic out at the time it happened."

Oh, wow. At Christmas time, too? That poor family. Wait... why did I say family!? What is wrong with me?

The instructor, Ray, had been teaching the alcohol awareness program for fifteen years. He was a recovering alcoholic and drug addict, and like many recovering addicts, he had felt the calling to help others. He was a skinny man in his early sixties; however the years of heavy abuse had rendered him ageless. He could be two hundred years old, for all Huckleberry knew.

Ray was good at his job. He may have had problems with his hearing, but he could always tell when someone was lying. He understood the weight of addiction, and it gave him foresight into what many folks were going through. He understood forgiveness. He understood recidivism. He understood struggle. He was a good man.

Huckleberry Gary liked Ray; and even though he, himself, wasn't an alcoholic, after the eight weeks of classes, he too, felt empathy for the plight of the addicted. It was an eye opening experience. There were six other classmates, all different ages, all different stories, but one common problem.

Huck liked Ray because he was genuine. He felt that Ray was honest and open and truly wanted to help the world, but Huck just couldn't shake the notion that there was a terrible darkness in Ray's past. Maybe he was finally going to get the answers he had been waiting for.

"I had been out on my delivery route and was just finishing up…" Ray paused before continuing with a smirk, "…a bottle of vodka."

The class let out a featherweight laughter to contrast the heaviness in the room.

"I had taken the exit to get back onto the highway and head back this way. However, if you are familiar with that exit, then you know it does a huge loop and splits into both directions." He began to sketch his route along the crudely drawn map on the whiteboard. "I didn't realize that I had missed my turn and was driving down the wrong side of the highway until it was too late."

Huck had given his complete attention now. He felt a ball inside his stomach. *Ho-ly shit! This guy is a murderer!*

"I had made it probably four miles before it happened," Ray continued. "There was a cop sitting beside a billboard. He saw me and instantly hit the lights. I was pulled over and immediately taken to jail. Luckily, no one got hurt."

"OH, COME ON!" Huck let out with disappointed frustration. The rest of the class turned toward him, with disdain in their eyes. "I mean," Huckleberry Gary gently corrected, "Thank goodness no one was hurt, obviously. I just felt that… I don't know. It was just an underwhelming ending to the story. I was expecting something else to happen… A little drama maybe? Forget it."

The class sat there in silence. Ray walked back to his seat.

"Just because no one was hurt, doesn't mean it wasn't a stupid and dangerous outcome from stupid and dangerous choices," Ray explained, "Your situation wasn't so different."

"No one was hurt with me, either," he defended himself.

"Your friend broke his collarbone, didn't he?" Ray asked.

"It was a hairline fracture. He's fine. It'll be stronger after it heals," Huck said.

"And your cousin?"

"Not my fault at all! Who puts a finger that close to a lone raccoon?! Also, a lone raccoon, bro? You can't trust a lone raccoon... you know there's got to be others around. They're social creatures, ya know," Huck said.

"Didn't you say that someone has an eye patch now?" Ray asked.

"Yeah, but in all fairness, I'm pretty sure that happened before we even got into the golf cart."

******

Huckleberry Gary left class and felt good about his journey in life. He knew who he was. He knew that he cared about humanity and felt pride in that. He would gladly pay his court fees and happily do his time. Everyone needs to hug the cactus now and then. But one thing he wouldn't do was change, and he certainly wasn't going to quit drinking. He needed it. He hunted shape-shifting-lizard-people for crying out loud. What more did they want from him?

He decided that his patrol would take him north along the river today. He hopped on his beach cruiser and pedaled home to grab his gear.

Life in Kenton could be hard on some people. The smallest differences in the world could make you feel like an outsider. Huck always felt a little different going through life. He never knew any romantic love, and he didn't know what it was like to be in the spotlight, to be celebrated. He joined the navy out of high school in hopes that he would find the community that he always wanted, but once there, he only felt like more of an outsider. He couldn't blame anyone, and was generally a pretty happy guy. He knew that people were still just tribal beasts deep down, and to be human was just the effort to out-think our instincts. The marginalized seek comfort with the marginalized, so oftentimes they leave towns like this in search of a tribe of their own. Everyone needs community.

Huck parked his bike in front of his apartment building, ran inside, and grabbed his gear. He lived in a small apartment complex in the historic downtown district of Kenton. The architecture was full of ornate carvings and beautiful, old windows. A large park sat in the center of the district where, during the summer, the city would put on events. They had blues bands and art shows. There was the annual bazaar. Attendance was always low, though. It seemed that many people would rather sit at home and watch Netflix, all the while complaining that there was never anything to do in a dead-end town like this.

The river bank was about a mile away, so Huckleberry Gary got to pedaling. There were maybe four hours left of sunlight on this perfect day, and he didn't want to waste it.

Cool air bounced off the water as Huck locked his bike to a tree. He grabbed a long hiking stick and began to walk up the trail toward the bluffs. He was nearing the edge of town and came close to the old Star-Lite Motel. There were always vacancies at the Star-Lite. It was an old single level motel with a dirt parking lot and a community charcoal grill outside that Huck figured hadn't been lit in years. A freshly washed Lexus was parked near one of the doors. A man came outside and grabbed a bag from the backseat. Gary recognized him from the trees. It was Doctor Anderson. He was the oncologist at the hospital. He was the doctor who worked with Huck's grandpa when he was diagnosed with cancer.

Another car drove past the motel and turned in behind it. A woman walked around the building with a bag in her hand. Huckleberry Gary didn't recognize her, but she was put together well. She had on heels and was wearing expensive looking sunglasses. She knocked on his motel room and when the door opened, the two embraced and began to kiss. The woman closed the door leaving everything left to the imagination. *Interesting.* Huckleberry Gary didn't know him well, but from what he remembered, the good doctor was a married man. *It's getting a little Grey's Anatomy here in good old Kenton, Illinois.*

Gary cracked on down the path. He walked through the woods between the motel and the river and came onto a small game trail that led along the river. He walked about half a mile before the path led away from the river and toward the road. It was peaceful. The Villa Leila appeared on the bluffs above him.

A truck cruised along the road heading toward town. Huck recognized Theo as he went by, not noticing him in the woods. The sun was beginning to set and his flask was empty. It was time to pack it up. Huckleberry Gary took a good look at the bluffs, and turned around to head home.

TWENTY

Theo pulled into the driveway of his father's house to find another car already there. *Now what?* The sun had finally set and the evening was upon them. Theo stepped out of the truck and approached the vehicle. A man stepped out and offered his hand. Theo didn't recognize Dino.

"Hello, my name is Dino Perez. I'm hoping to speak with Abner Beckett. This still his place?" he said to Theo as Theo shook his hand.

"Well sir, I'm afraid you're about four days too late. He passed away on Sunday. I'm Theo. I'm his son. I'm just here cleaning out the place and making arrangements and all that fun stuff."

Dino looked surprised.

"Is there something I can help you with?" Theo asked.

"Oh...I'm sorry for your loss. I didn't realize," Dino said.

"Thank you. It's no biggie. What can I do for you?" Theo said.

"Well," Dino began, "this may be weird for you... but I had some questions for him, about the day his wife... your mom... was killed."

"My mother was killed in a car wreck. I'm not sure what else happened. Just that I was in her belly and I survived, but she didn't."

"Car wreck?" Dino said.

"Yeah," Theo said.

"Is there any way I could maybe look around a bit? Maybe some old photos around that time... any journals or diaries?" Dino asked.

Theo laughed. "I don't think you knew my father that well. He wasn't the type to keep a diary," he said.

"Any death records?"

"Isn't that something a detective would have an easier way of finding than me? What is it that you want to know?" There was suspicion in Theo's voice.

"Theo, this probably isn't my place... but your mother didn't die in a car accident. She was murdered," Dino said.

Theo was completely stupefied. His father wasn't even buried yet and was still, somehow, keeping him at bay.

"Murdered?" Theo couldn't understand. The news sent a jolt into his stomach.

"What did your father tell you about your mom's death?" Dino asked.

Theo stood there in shock. Everything he thought he knew about his birth was a lie. He was burning with questions. He was lost. He was totally alone.

"Do you want a beer, Mr. Perez?" he asked.

"Sure."

Dino noticed Theo's limp as he was led through the garage and into the kitchen. Theo opened the fridge and pulled out two cans of light beer. He cracked one open and poured it into a glass, offering it to Dino. He cracked the other and drank straight from the can.

"You're gonna have to give me some details here, man," Theo said. "This is all pretty overwhelming."

Dino began by telling him the story. He explained that he was a detective on the case. It was a late night, and his parents were out taking a walk when they were attacked. His father claimed it was a man with a hood over his head. They mugged them and stabbed his mother through the stomach. To save the baby's life, they had to perform an emergency surgery.

Theo understood why his father would keep that from him as a kid, but Theo had been a grown man for years and couldn't figure why he was never let in on this.

"I can't believe it," Theo said.

"Well, I'm sorry to be the one to give you all of this," Dino offered. His days with the Kenton Detective Unit had given him a lot of experience in delivering strange news to people, but it had been a long time, and Dino was a little rusty.

"So, Theo, when did you get to town?" the old man asked.

"Sunday afternoon," Theo answered.

Dino found this to be a coincidence. The killings, if you count turtle-slaughter, began Monday night. It wasn't much of one, but he learned that you never throw a coincidence away, no matter how small.

"What have you been up to since being back? Enjoying yourself?"

"I guess as much as one can in this situation. Just been cleaning the house and catching up with old friends," Theo answered.

"I see, and what did you get up to last night? Do anything?" Dino asked.

"Well, I was at the bar," Theo answered with some reluctance.

"What bar?"

"Cherry Street…"

"And where were you around midnight?" Dino asked.

"I was walking home from the bar…" Theo's reluctance quickly shifted to annoyance. He began to feel as though he was being interrogated.

"Safe move. Don't want to be drinking and driving. So were you alone on your walk home?" Dino figured the route in his head. Theo walked through the very area of the old lady's house the same night she was murdered.

"Yeah, I was alone… Can I ask what this has to do with anything?" Theo asked.

"Oh, I'm just trying to make friendly conversation. Nothing important," Dino said.

"Okay, well I still have a lot of cleaning to do so if there's nothing else I can do for you…"

"No, I appreciate the time. Thanks for the beer." Dino finished the glass and set it next to the sink.

Theo led him to the door. They shook hands and Dino walked toward the car before turning around. "If there's anything you find or think of that could shed a little more light on things, please let me know," Dino said with a smile.

Theo nodded and waved. Dino backed out of the driveway and noticed the dirty truck Theo had been driving. The back of the truck was covered with white dust. He had been out on the gravel roads. He's been out by the river. Dino thought that maybe he should keep an eye on Theo Beckett, but now he needed to find Damian, the River Rat.

TWENTY-ONE

Dr. Anderson opened the door to his room at the Star-Lite Motel with a desperately exaggerated swagger of a British spy. There was a woman standing there waiting on him. She was holding a bottle of cabernet and two plastic wine glasses by the stem. It was starting to get darker and the one solitary light in the parking lot was surrounded by an eclipse of moths, refusing to give in to the cool fall weather.

"Well, hello Doctor. Can I help you?" Dr. Anderson asked.

"Shut up," the woman laughed. She entered the room, and the two embraced. They didn't even get the bottle of wine open before they were making love on the squeaky mattress. The two used to prefer the term: coitus, until one night when Dr. Anderson, in the throes of sexual desire, yelled out the words "Coitus me, baby!" Since then, medical terminology stayed clear of the bedroom.

The woman's name was Dr. Lindsay Prynne, a third year resident at the hospital. She couldn't quite figure out what it was about Dr. Anderson that she found so attractive. He wasn't a good looking man, nor was he all that charming, but he was sweet and capable and the complete opposite of her husband. She thought at first that it was the forbidden romance that was so alluring, but it had been going on for almost two years, and she now found herself madly in love with the man.

She rolled over to her back and stared at the ceiling, breathing heavily and happily. Dr. Anderson stood up, walked to the sink, and returned with a glass of water. She smiled and took a long drink.

"I told her," Dr. Anderson said as he sat back down on the bed.

"What?" she asked. She wasn't sure how to respond to that.

"It's done," he continued. "I'm moving out at the end of the month. My brother is going to let me stay with him until I find a place, unless we…"

"I'll tell him this week..," she interrupted. "It's going to break his heart."

"We can't keep doing this," Dr. Anderson said.

Lindsay knew it was time. It wasn't fair, but life is messy. She couldn't keep up the charade any longer.

"I'll tell him this week," she repeated.

"You've been saying that for months now," Dr. Anderson said.

"I'll do it," she said. "I love you. I want to be with you."

There was a loud slam against the wall, where the back of the motel reached the woods. The couple froze. Another bang shook the room. Dr. Anderson stood up and got dressed quickly. He crept toward the window. There was nothing outside. He moved toward the front door.

"What the hell..?" he said.

"What are you doing?!" Dr. Prynne asked. She stood up and followed his lead, getting dressed as fast as she could.

"There is someone out there… Where is your phone? Call the police," he said.

Lindsay grabbed her phone to dial but stopped herself before completing the call. If she called the police, then they would be caught for sure. She wasn't ready for that. She wanted to be the one to tell her husband, not the police. Not like this.

"Just wait a second," she said. "Don't go out there! Let's just think about this."

"It's probably a bear or something," Dr. Anderson offered.

"A bear?! Why on earth would you go outside if there's a bear out there?" she said.

Another slam rattled the room, this time down the building toward the road, away from the room.

"See," Dr. Prynne said. "It's moving away."

A sense of relief came over Dr. Anderson. "You know, you make a good point. What on earth was I thinking? I was going to go outside? That's like, the dumbest thing I could have done," he said. "What am I going to do? Fight a bear? That's crazy."

Before he could fully unpack his poor decision making, the old motel door crashed open sending splinters of rotted wood all around the room. Dr. Prynne screamed as the creature burst through the door, dripping water on the musty carpet. Dr. Anderson fell backward from fear and landed on his back. He began to crabwalk away screaming. The monster followed slowly. Water dripped from the tip of the blade fused to his right hand.

Dr. Prynne threw the empty bottle of wine at the creature. It bounced off of his head with no effect. The monster turned to her, studied her for a moment, and continued toward the man.

Dr. Anderson made his way to the kitchenette but hit his head against the cabinets. There was nowhere else to go. He was trapped. The creature held one foot down on his chest leaving the heart exposed. Water dripped on Dr. Anderson's face, mixing with the salty tears. The blade made its way into his chest, slicing through his heart, and leaving him only moments left to live. He looked back at Dr. Prynne. She was frozen in fear. Life left his body easily.

The monster turned away from the man, gave one long look at Dr. Prynne, and then moved out of the door with its broken movement.

Dr. Prynne shook herself out of the shock that she was in. She snatched up her things as fast as she could and ran for her life.

TWENTY-TWO

Dino walked through the doors of the Cherry Street Tavern like he was walking into a lion's den. He hadn't stepped foot into a bar like this in a long time. Back when he was a cop, he would never go out to some tavern of ill repute. It was too risky. Instead he would opt for the cop bar in town, the Elk's Club. It's hard being a cop in the real world. People act differently around you. Everyone thinks they're about to get busted for something, and they're not that wrong. Everyone is guilty of something.

It was just after dinner, and the sun had set. A DJ sporting a rat-tail and a pair of overalls was busy hooking up some over-sized speakers in the corner. Wednesday nights were the official karaoke nights at the tavern. It had a regular following. People would swarm the bar at 9:00 p.m., nearly drunk and eager to sign up for their regular song. Old Man Frank would usually be the first to sign up and, to his credit, did a pretty decent job with "My Way." He was proud to share the same moniker as Ol' Blue Eyes himself, but to his chagrin, he did not share the same buttery voice.

Dino approached the bar. A young black man with long dreadlocks was cleaning a few pint glasses. Some of the local rednecks in town referred to him as "that Jamaican dude." He would often work that angle and give out a couple "jah's" and "tank you badda, you walk good now's" all while laughing on the inside and watching his tip bucket fill to the rim. He figured why not? Just lean into it. His name was actually Dominic, and he was born just across the river in Missouri. He was a hell of a duck hunter.

"Excuse me. I'm looking for a man named Damian. Know him?" Dino asked the bartender.

"Oh, you're in at the right time. He hasn't yet pissed himself," Dominic pointed to a table near the jukebox. A man with slouched shoulders was staring at nothing through the window.

"Thanks." Dino left a dollar on the bar.

"Irie…"

Damian, the River Rat was sitting with his back to the bar. He was wearing a mismatched camouflage jacket and pants. Like, if he was walking around the woods in the springtime, some confused turkey would think to himself, *holy shit, a floating torso!*

"Damian?" Dino approached the man. He turned around and looked at Dino with a confused furrow in his brows. His eyes were glazed with despair.

"I'm, uh…Detective Perez," Dino was technically lying, but it felt good saying it.

"Did you find it?!" For a moment Damian's eyes lit up.

"It?" Dino asked.

"You know," Damina slurred. "The monster."

"No… but we are still working on it. I had some different questions for you." Dino sat down and leaned in and set his phone on the table to record the conversation. He asked Damian about the night his dear turtle was murdered. Damian recounted the night. He explained AND told him about the she-devil bartender that slammed his head on the bar. He mentioned his walk home. He omitted the "bush lites."

Dino asked him to describe the creature.

"He looked like a man, but not a man from this world," Damian explained. "He was covered in moss and had dark rubbery skin and ragged clothes that were ripped apart. He looked like a zombie! Like a river zombie! His hand was a long bladed rusted knife that was like it was his hand. His eyes were black. He moved like he didn't know how to walk…"

"Like a limp?" Dino asked.

"Well, I guess so, sure. It was like he was possessed by something else. Something evil…"

"Go on..," Dino said.

"He broke through my door and threw me against the wall. I landed on my coffee table and rolled into the TV that my new TV sat on top of. It was blurry. I broke my bong…er…uh flower vase. Then, just when I thought the monster was going to put an end to me, he grabbed my sweet buddy, Gustav, and stabbed him through his perfect little turtle heart," Damian explained.

"I'm sorry. So this man, he had a knife?" Dino said.

"Yeah… but it was a part of him. Like, his fingers were the blade. It wasn't human. I'm telling ya. It was the devil… well maybe not *the* devil… but they have to know each other."

"After this, where did it go? Did you see any headlights?" Dino asked.

"No, it just left through the broken door. I didn't chase it!"

"It could have had a boat..," Dino said to himself.

"I didn't hear no boat," Damian said. "It was a monster."

Damian finished the last of his beer and set the glass down on the table. Dino picked up his phone and thanked him. He left the bar and decided to take a walk around the neighborhood and clear his mind. He thought about what the River Rat had mentioned about the way the monster moves. *It moves funny. Like it walks with a limp. Theo Beckett walks with a limp.*

******

It was midnight and Captain Russell walked underneath the crime scene tape and into the opened motel room. One of the officers was questioning the owner of the building just outside. Another was taking pictures of the room. A blanket was carefully laid over the lifeless body of Doctor Anderson. Clothes were thrown about the room, and the mattress was flipped over. It looked like there was a hell of a fight before all this went down.

"Well, this is an interesting turn of events," Captain Ross said to anyone listening. He crouched down and examined the body. There was one clean stab wound to the heart. He covered the body back up and stood. "So what do we have here? Anything good?" Captain Russell asked.

"There's nothing good about this. Victim's name is Dr. Benjamin Anderson. He's an oncologist at the hospital. The door was smashed in. There's only one working camera on premises, and that's in the office. There's no murder weapon. We got no hair, we got nothing. There's a few footprints in the dirt to the door, but they disappear into the woods," Detective Carol Shelly said. She was tired. This was the third murder victim in two days. The KDU had been so busy with crime scenes that they'd barely had time to analyze what little clues they had.

"Who else was here?" Captain Ross looked around.

"As far as we can see, the doc was here alone. We figured maybe he just needed a time out away from people. Makes barely any sense, but I don't see any evidence of another person. There's only one glass of wine..." Detective Shelly shrugged her shoulders.

They walked outside together. Captain Russell examined the foot prints. They were faint. Whoever it was didn't have any shoes on. The dirt around the prints was beginning to dry, but there was evidence that it was wet, like footprints on the beach after a swim.

The other officer was questioning the motel owner near the front door to the office. Captain Ross and Detective Shelly walked across the dirt parking lot and joined them.

"Was there anyone with the doctor when they checked in?" the captain asked the motel owner.

"No, like I said to this lovely man... he checked in alone. Very nice man. You know, I could have been a doctor. I thought about medical school, but I just didn't want to limit myself... my ma sai..," the motel owner said.

"Honestly man, has anyone ever come to this motel to stay... alone?" Captain Ross interrupted.

"What are you inferring, sir? This is a classy joint! We even clean the comforters..." The owner was offended.

"Come on..," Captain Ross said.

"Okay, fine. We don't always clean the comforters, but if they need it, we do it."

"Need it?" the other officer jumped in.

"Like if there's a stain or something on it…"

"Jesus Christ," Detective Shelly said.

"I'm not talking about the damned comforters. I don't care. Let's not lose focus here. Do you ever see anyone renting a room here alone?" Captain Ross asked.

"Oh, right. Nope, never. We are the number one destination for the local daytime hookers, and the all-too-occasional *rendezvous secret*..," the owner hung his head in shame. "This is my hill to die on, I suppose. My legacy."

"There were two towels on the floor..," Captain Russell said. "We need to find out who else was here, and I'm guessing it wasn't his wife."

Detective Shelly nodded in agreement. She turned to the owner. "Let's go take a look at the camera footage," she said to the man.

"Yes, yes, no problem," he answered. "But just to be clear, I already asked this dude, er… officer, but I wanted to circle back… There's no need to, like, dig into any financial information right? I mean, it's all clean and everything. Tight as a fucking drum, honestly! But, my tax guy is out of town currently and I…"

"Just the camera footage for now," Shelly offered.

"Cool cool cool," the motel owner said.

TWENTY-THREE

Theo and Heather were drinking coffee and going through his dad's basement. They had divided the room into sections: Sell, donate, keep, or burn. So far, the "donate" section was winning. It was about ten in the morning, and things were moving along. Heather held up an old TV tray and showed it to Theo. It was covered with Batman stickers that were peeling away with time.

"What about this? This is a gem. We can't sell it... you can't put a price on this relic. I didn't know you were a Batman fan?" Heather prodded.

"I was a sticker fan... still am," Theo responded. "Donate it."

"I'm keeping it," Heather said. She tossed it into her own personal pile by the stairs. So far, it was full of old books and clothes.

Theo uncovered a shelf full of old shoes. Some hadn't been worn in thirty years. Theo never understood the need to hold on to items from the past. You can't take it with you. Unless you want to be buried with it, but even that seems futile.

"Jesus, look at all of this. Why do people keep all of these things? All these pack rats do is hold on to shit for other people to move around," Theo said.

"I love it!" Heather said. "There's stories behind all of this stuff!"

"What's the story behind these?" Theo held up a pair of very old flip flops covered in pink flamingos.

"OH MY GOD! Suzi would love those!" Heather snatched them out of his hands and placed them very carefully on the top of her pile. "I can't believe I'm about to marry a woman..," Heather said.

She had dated a few men over the years, but Suzi was the first woman. It was an interesting change in her world. Growing up, the church was such an integral part of her life. She felt conflicted during the first year with Suzi. She was worried about sin, but just couldn't change who she fell in love with, nor did she want to. It was a paradox.

"Suzi is amazing. I can believe *you'd* want to put a ring on that," Theo answered. "I just can't believe *she* is willing to go along with it!"

"What? You kidding me? I'm gonna be a trophy wife!" Heather said.

"I'm going to get drunk and catch the bouquet..," Theo laughed.

"You think God hates me?" she asked.

"Probably."

"Good lord, it must be exhausting being you…" Heather tossed an old magazine at him.

"Hey!" Theo was moving the shoes off of the shelf and didn't see it coming. He lost his balance and almost fell over.

"No, come on. I don't think God gives a shit who we choose to spend our lives with," he said after regaining his composure.

"Yeah, me neither. It bothered me so much at first, but once we met each other's parents and everyone got along so well, I didn't really think too much about it," Heather said.

"There you go... you can't change who you love. Why would God use love as a weapon?" Theo said.

"Did you love Caroline... when you guys got married?" Heather asked.

"Yeah...Sure. I think so? It's all such a blurry whirlwind of memory and time, I can't really remember how I felt back then. Just how I feel now... like I'm burned out. When we got married, I remember having doubts, but I thought that was normal..."

"It is," Heather said.

"...But Saylor was already four or five, and it felt like maybe we had skipped a step, so we got married. It felt right at the time... like we completed each other. Jerry Maguire style, baby... but the more I think back on it, the more I realize that we just made each other more and more incomplete."

"But you got Saylor so can't be a waste, right?" Heather said.

"Yep. It all works out in the end," Theo stepped off the ladder.

"Suzi bought me a ring," Heather said.

"Oh shit?! Let's see that bad Larry," Theo said as he set down a box he was moving.

"I can't bring myself to put it on, it feels strange," she said as she pulled a ring out from her pocket and showed Theo. It was a small ring. It looked old, with a small diamond on it. Theo held it up to the light, pretending to be a jeweler. Heather laughed and snagged it back from him.

"Oh, that looks like a lesbian ring, for sure," he said.

"I will beat you to death with this… thing?" Heather held an old pool noodle.

Theo laughed and continued pulling shoes off the shelf. There were old duck boots and a couple pairs of white sneakers. Theo reached up and pulled down an old pair of hiking boots and noticed one of them was missing a shoelace. He set the pair down. Behind them was a smaller pair of shoes. They were an old pair of women's sneakers. They must have belonged to his mother, he thought. Theo grabbed them with care and took a good look at them. He noticed that one of them was also missing a shoelace.

"Weird," Theo said.

"What's weird?" Heather asked.

"These shoes are missing shoelaces," Theo answered.

"WHAT?! HOLY SHIT. FOR REAL?"

"It's weird..," Theo said, ignoring her sarcasm.

"Why is that so weird?" Heather asked.

"Well… because I think I know where they are."

TWENTY-FOUR

Dino's garage had morphed into an office. Empty coffee mugs and a short pile of dirty plates sat on the workbench. A radio was playing pop hits in the background. There were case files now lined up on the wall, and a big map of the area with pins showing the 1986 murders alongside the sightings from today. Dino noticed that the murders were in similar places, all along the river near the bluffs, beneath the Villa Leila.

"Hurt people hurt people," Dino said to himself studying the file from Winona Beckett's death. Hers was the last in the series of monster sightings, yet Abner claimed that it was a hooded man that did it. Then, just as mysteriously as they began, they stopped. *Did the killer move on to another location?* Dino couldn't put the pieces together, but he felt in his gut that Abner Beckett knew more than he let on.

But Abner Beckett is dead... and the murders began again. Abner Beckett's son came home... and the murders began again.

He looked through the file on Mary Ann's mother. *The monster moves funny. Theo Beckett has an injured leg. Theo Beckett moves funny. He has no alibi, and was in fact, in the same area around the same time as the murder.*

"Hurt people hurt people," he repeated.

His cell phone vibrated on the workbench and nearly fell off the corner. Dino caught it midair and answered. The caller ID read KDU.

"Captain Russell..," Dino said. "I'll bring the files back soon, the copier was down…"

"Dino," the captain began. "I can't believe I'm going to say this, but is there any way you could stop by today? I think we have something you may want to see."

"Sure, what is it?" Dino asked.

"We have some video from the Star-Lite, and…, well, I could use your insight here." The captain had a sense of frustration in his voice.

"I'll head right there," Dino said.

He hung up the phone and put it in his pocket, grabbed his keys, and left the garage.

******

The captain stood behind the chair of Detective Shelly. They were both in silence watching the grainy footage on a computer screen when Dino walked in.

"What's going on?" Dino asked.

"Dino," Captain Russell said as he turned around. "Thank you for coming back."

Dino approached them and took a look at the screen. There was a fuzzy black and white picture of the dirt parking lot at the Star-Lite Motel. The angle was tilted a bit, and you could barely see the rooms on the side of the screen. Giant white orbs of light were floating in the foreground.

"These damn moths…," Detective Shelly said.

"Take a look at this," Captain Russell said to Dino. He moved out of the way and allowed Dino a better view.

Detective Shelly hit play, and the orbs of light came to life, flickering around the street light above the shoddily placed security camera.

A car pulled up in the top corner of the screen. A woman steps out and walks around the car and up to the door, her head just out of frame. She stands there until the door opens. Dino couldn't make out who was on the other end of the door.

"Who is it?" Dino asked.

"Just wait," Captain Russell answered.

The woman entered the room. Shelly hit the fast forward button. It moved ahead a little over two hours. She hit play. Dino put his face closer to the screen. The bugs had cleared out, and there was a better view. He couldn't believe it when he saw it.

The creature came into screen with its broken movements. It creeps to the same door that the woman had entered and busts it open with ease. It enters the room. Detective Shelly hit the pause button.

"Jesus…," Dino said.

"It's real…," Captain Russell couldn't believe the words he was saying.

A few minutes after, the monster left the room and moved across the dirt, its head just out of screen as well. The grainy film made it hard to work out the details, but Dino leaned in close. Shortly after the creature left, the woman darted out of the room holding her things. She jumped into her car and reversed it further than necessary to get out of the parking lot. They froze the film.

"Look at that. Her license plate," Shelly said. She wrote down the information.

"Back it up," Dino said. He couldn't care less about the woman. He was finally seeing something that had been plaguing him for the better part of his life. Shelly rewound it back to the monster leaving the room and paused it. It was in mid step. It had ratted pants and an old torn up shirt and had a knife in its hand. *It's a man?*

"The Creature from the Mississippi. I can't believe it's real. Dino, I owe you an apology. I..." Captain Russell began.

"You don't owe me a thing, Captain. That's no creature. That's just a man. A sick and dangerous man," Dino said. *And I know exactly who that man is.*

THE TREASURE OF THURSDAY

TWENTY-FIVE

1962

Gray Dougal woke up with sand in his crack. The northern Sahara desert was beginning to heat up, and the tiny particles felt cool to the skin. He sat up and banged his boots together before putting them on. A rogue scorpion had taught him this valuable lesson a few weeks back. Always bang your boots before putting them on. He stood up and loomed over his best friend, Carson, who stirred on his cot below him. Gray gave him a light kick.

"Come on," he said. "We're getting closer."

Gray opened the canvas flap and stepped outside and into the morning. His dusty brown hair was sticking up on the sides. He stretched his arms behind his back as he looked out toward the rolling dunes of the Sahara glowing pink in the east, an ocean of shapes and stories. The sun had little left below the horizon, and the cool desert night was soon to be forgotten. Carson stood from his makeshift bed, and they began to pack up their things.

"Three months wandering through Africa. Two weeks in the mindless desert. This better be worth it. And I better not die! "Carson said as he loaded his bags onto the back of a camel.

"Look at the bright side, buddy." Gray smiled as he wrapped a shemagh around his face. "Treasure or not, what an experience!"

"Banana beer in Kigali... That was an experience. The girls in Cape Town... That was an experience," Carson said. "Two weeks in the Sahara... I'm ready for the next experience."

Gray let out a belly laugh. He rolled up the tent and slung it over his shoulders. "Just think of all the experiences we can have when we find this gold!" he said.

"Oh, it's gold today is it? Yesterday it was jewels," Carson said.

"The Treasure of Thursday!" Gray said. "What day is it?"

"Oh man, I left my calendar in my other tent," Carson answered. "No idea."

The pair had been best friends since childhood. They met on a little league team after Carson had moved to Kenton. His parents thought it would help him make friends. It was hard being the new kid in town. When Gray took the chance to be friendly, it was a relief to both Carson and his parents. Since then, the two had been almost inseparable. A friendship like theirs often stole traits from other types of relationships. They would argue like they were an old married couple. They would keep each other's secrets safe like they were brothers. They would back each other up in a fight even if the other was in the wrong. It was an honest and angry kind of love, but love all the same.

After Gray had graduated from college, but before accepting his destiny and beginning his hand me down position within the family business, he decided he would burn up some of his trust fund early and take a holiday in Africa. He had always wanted to visit the dark continent. He remembered seeing photos of Theodore Roosevelt on his African expedition, and felt that same call to adventure in his own heart. It was something that he couldn't shake. He had to go.

His parents agreed on a three week vacation, so he bought two tickets to Cairo and convinced his best friend to quit his job at the machine shop and join him on the trip of a lifetime. Carson was reluctant. He, unlike Gray, did not come from a wealthy family. He didn't have the option to go to college. He didn't have a trust fund to burn. However, he did have a few gin and tonics, which assisted Gray in convincing his best friend to join him on the adventure of a lifetime.

They arrived in Cape Town and did what most young men would do. They headed straight for a bar. They would be heading northeast in the morning, with a goal of seeing as much of the continent as possible, so this night was their only night in Cape Town, and was to be a party to remember.

After things closed down, and they made their way from the bar to their rented room, they stumbled upon an old man in an alley. He was rambling on about a treasure. The old man was certain that there was a cache of gold high in the Atlas Mountains of Morocco; a fortune just waiting to be discovered on the other side of the continent. Gray was not the type of person to ignore destiny when he heard it. He listened to the man closely.

"I saw him!" the man said to Carson, as they walked through the alley.

"Who did you see?" Carson asked.

"But I had not the right colors. I had no green. I had no white," the old man slurred.

"Oh yeah? That's too bad. Come on. We will help you get home." The boys walked with the old man.

"The gold, buried deep somewhere on Mount Toubkal, the highest peak in North Africa. Nothing higher. At the end of a deep gorge, beside a waterfall… but you cannot go there. Kaafir are not allowed," the old man told them.

"What is Kaafir?" Gray asked.

"*You* are Kaafir," the old man said.

"Oh, that's too bad," Gray said.

"Kanz Alkhamis…" the old man said. He sat down on the ground against the wall.

"Where do you live?" Gray asked the man.

"I almost had it. Now I can never be free. Kanz Alkhamis…," he repeated.

"Sir, where do you live?" Gray asked again.

"Here. I live right here," the old man lay down to try to pass out. Gray took his coat off and gave it to the man.

"Do not trust the black owl. He will only bring you pain," the man began to drift asleep.

"Come on," Carson put his hand on Gray's shoulder. "Let's get back to our room."

Weeks later, at a café in Port Sudan, the two were having breakfast. It was a beautiful day. The salty air was blowing off of the Red Sea. Gray was distracted with a drawing that he made on his napkin. The owner of the café was refilling a cup of tea.

"Excuse me," Gray looked up and spoke to the man, "Would you help me with a translation?"

"Of course," the owner answered. He was a burly man in a white shirt and wearing a red fez. The small hat exaggerated his large head.

"What does Kanz Alkhamis mean?" Gray asked.

"Kanz Alkhamis? Oh, that would mean... I'm not sure how to say it... Thursday's Treasure."

"Thursday's Treasure," Carson repeated.

Gray thanked the man and turned to his best friend to show him the napkin.

"Look, so here's what I'm thinking," Gray held the napkin down from the wind. He had drawn a crude looking map through a scribbled looking mountain range. Gray wasn't the best artist.

"You're still thinking about this? What is this? You drew a treasure map?" Carson said.

"Yeah...Look here. I was looking through a real map of the Atlas Mountains earlier. Now there are two choices. There's a lake on the east side of Mount Toubkal, but a river runs through the west side. I say we head to Ouarzazate and follow the river through the mountains until we find a waterfall," Gray said.

"This is not how you get a treasure map!" Carson said.

"Says who?" Gray asked.

"Says who? Says every treasure hunting story ever told. You have to find a map on a dead body or in an old tomb or something. You don't draw your own on an old nasty napkin!"

"Well, we haven't found an old tomb or a dead body," Gray said. "This was my only option."

"Exactly. We didn't find an old tomb or a dead body. We found an old drunk guy... half way across the continent. We can't just cross the desert in the hopes that an old drunk guy half way across the continent was telling us correct information on a mystical hidden treasure," Carson said.

"Sure we can!"

"Look, our flight is in the morning. I have to find a job. We can't just stay in Africa looking for the 'Treasure of Thursday' which is also, by the way, the lamest name of a treasure ever. May as well be called 'The Treasure of Not-Quite-Friday.'"

"What are you talking about? This is awesome! This is our quest, man! We can do this! We will be rich!" Gray said.

"You're already rich!" Carson said.

"Okay. You'll be rich. I'll just be…rich…er."

Carson looked at his friend. Gray was always so carefree. He wasn't used to hearing the word 'no' and if so, he was often able to turn it to a 'yes'. Carson didn't come from money, and growing up with Gray around was always a constant reminder of that. He never understood why some kids had everything, while most had nothing.

"Just give me one month in Africa?" Gray smiled.

"No," Carson said.

"Two weeks..," Gray said.

"Gray… I can't,"

"Two weeks. Come on, man. Think about it. You'll have the rest of your life to do whatever job you gotta do when we get back, but today… right now, we have a chance to do something so incredibly stupid, that it might just pay off..," Gray said.

"Two weeks?" Carson said.

"No less, no more," Gray said.

"Goddammit... Fine."

"Yes!" Gray said. "Let's go get some camels."

"What? Camels? Why can't we just fly?"

"Well, that's the thing... Since we were only supposed to be here for three weeks... Well, buddy, we're almost out of money. No big deal though. We'll be fine. We'll find a job. It's only two weeks."

Three months later, there they were, standing just outside of Ouarzazate, Morocco, desert-hardened and five thousand miles closer to destiny.

TWENTY-SIX

Young Love is the most envied of all the many kinds of love. Old Love and Bitter Love and all the others are helpless against it. They can only watch as Young Love does its backflips on the trampoline. Its knees without pops as it walks. It knows nothing of the sciatic nerve. It's just fast and shiny and impulsive and willing to drink poison at the drop of a hat. How can any other love compete with that?

Neither Gray nor Leila knew what they were in for when they met, but when they did their lives would be forever changed.

Ouarzazate, the doorway to the desert, lied smack dab in between the green and plentiful Atlas Mountains and the dry and unforgiving Sahara Desert. The city is an enigma, with a devil on one shoulder and an angel on the other. The beautiful kindness of Islam danced among the thieves and eager desert guides, ready to take whatever money the adventure-fueled tourist is willing to give for the chance to test their meddle in the outskirts of the Sahara.

The marketplace in Ouarzazate was buried in rich colors. Fabrics lined the backs of the many stalls, in contrast with the plain white linen clothing of the owner as he tried to sell his wares to the passing by pedestrians. Smells of roasted lamb and cumin floated through the air. The sun reflected off the sandy colored buildings.

Gray and Carson were clinging to the distant shadows, window shopping. They were doing their best to avoid the heat, a heat that you never get used to.

"We're broke," Carson said, looking off into the bazaar.

"I know," Gray answered. They had sold their camels and had just enough money to get some food for a few days, but they would soon be busted. "We need to find some work."

Carson unbuttoned the last button from the bottom of his shirt, exposing his torso. They had been beaten by the desert for months. Their faces were red, and they both needed a shave. Gray stood up, ran a hand through his matted hair, and took a risky sniff of the armpit. He then left the safety of the shade toward the bazaar.

"Where are you going?" Carson called after him.

"I'm tired of stinking. I'm going to find a job so I can find a room so I can take a shower!" he called back.

Gray meandered through the different stalls, looking for anyone that seemed like they had more work than they could handle. He approached a few owners, but the language barrier proved difficult. English had been common throughout the country for years, but Ouarzazate was a little more off the beaten path than the more touristy areas, and it hadn't yet spread as deeply.

The sixties in Morocco had been a haven for the arts. Writers and musicians and actors had come to soak up the mystic powers of the desert. They would wear the traditional clothes and incorporate the traditional musical styles into their own. They would fall in love with the architecture and get tattoos. They made sure to get photos to prove they were there. It was growing dangerously close to becoming a fad. The Rolling Stones would take to Morocco like the Beatles to India. This is how art grows, through innocent theft.

King Hassan II had just come into power, a new constitution was being drawn, and Morocco was finding itself in yet another existential moment with its recent independence from its French protectorate. The Kingdom of Morocco had been born and was now learning to walk.

Gray made his way through the bazaar and found a stall selling produce. There was an older woman moving a heavy box of oranges. Gray approached her.

"I'll take one of those, please." Gray motioned toward the orange. The woman's face was covered, but her eyes smiled. She set the box down and gave him an orange. Gray paid her and smiled back. "Maybe that'll help lighten the load."

"It's one orange lighter, but I'm a few santimat heavier," she joked.

"Oh, thank God! You speak English?" Gray asked her.

"I do," she said. "A little."

"My friend and I just arrived. We are hoping to find some work," Gray said. "We need some help…"

The woman smiled and called into the back. "Leila!" she said.

A young woman, the same age as Gray, entered through the back door of the fruit stall. She was wearing a green djellaba that hung low, almost dragging behind her feet, and a similar mask as her mother. Her eyes locked with Gray's before her mother stole her attention. She spoke something in a language that Gray had never heard. Although he didn't speak Arabic, he had grown used to the sounds of it. This was not it.

Gray felt nerves poke into his stomach at the sight of the woman. She smelled like frankincense, and it only reminded him of how bad he smelled in comparison. He clenched his arms to his side tightly, in an effort to seal in the stench. His hair was most likely a mess, but he wasn't going to risk lifting his arms to fix it.

After a brief exchange with her mother, Leila left through the rear of the stall. The older woman turned back to Gray. "She is going to get my husband, her father. He could use the help picking fruit. He may have a job for you," she said.

Gray couldn't believe his luck. Fortune was finally on his side again.

******

Carson was lying on his back with his hat covering his face. The shade had shifted, and his feet were now sticking out into the sun. Gray tossed an orange on his stomach, startling him fully awake from his half-slumber.

"Come on," Gray said. "Let's get our things and get going."

Carson leaned on his side and began to unwrap his citrus gift. "Where to now, my liege?" he asked.

"I found us a place to stay," Gray answered. He put on his backpack.

"Where??" Carson said again.

"A fruit farm," Gray answered with a smile. He threw some gear over his shoulder. "Come on, now, quick march! We got some fruit to pick!"

TWENTY-SEVEN

The fruit farm was much larger than Gray had expected. There were fields of strawberries and mandarin trees lined the distance. Warehouses were spread around the compound, with large trucks being loaded with crates and sent on their way. Leila's father, Said, was giving the boys a short tour, explaining the business and their new role in it.

"Do you know what the biggest Moroccan export is?" Said asked.

"Sand?" Gray said. He looked to his best friend for a reaction. Carson ignored it and looked at the sky. Leila offered a giggle before her father shot her a disapproving look.

"We don't know," Carson said, in an effort to remain respectful. "Please, what is the biggest Moroccan export?"

"The biggest Moroccan export is..," Said said as he extended his arm showing off the fields, "Berries!"

They walked on as Said continued the tour of the compound. Gray and Carson were already sweating from the heat, but the gentle breeze was a welcome respite from their time in the desert. They went from field to field, talking about the crops. Said explained to them their duties. There wasn't much money involved, but Gray and Carson were offered a place to stay and three meals a day. It seemed like a deal too good to pass up.

Leila had excused herself and went back to the house to help her mother. Her father showed the boys to their room. It was in the back of one of the warehouses where there was a small table in the corner that held a generous meal for them. There were two cots against opposite walls and a small window that looked out toward the berries.

The showers, like most of the best things in life, were short lived, but with a belly full of food and clean sheets on comfy beds, the desert-worn men slept better than they had in weeks.

The next morning, Gray and Carson woke up, dressed, and got to work. They were in good spirits and took to the simple labor with ease. They picked the berries, loaded them into crates, and delivered them to the warehouse. The warehouse workers were quiet, and oftentimes didn't acknowledge Gray's nor Carson's existence. They would load the crates into trucks and head out on their deliveries.

With three warehouses on the compound, the farm was more of an export business than anything else. The trucks would be loaded with mandarins, grapefruits, lemons, and all kinds of berries. It was a flourishing business, and never a shortage of work.

The other pickers didn't talk much, though that was more due to the language barrier than their disposition. Over the weeks, Gray learned the Arabic words for the different crops. He learned to say please and thank you. He began to learn some of the names. There was one phrase that he couldn't figure out, but he was determined.

"Al himar yaemal bijohdin kabir alyawm," they would say and laugh.

"Himar yaemal bijohdin…?" Gray would ask.

"It means 'good job,'" one of them would say.

"Yes! That right. It mean 'good job!'" another would repeat.

"Nice," Gray would say. "Himar yaemal to you guys too!"

The warehouse workers had a different attitude than the pickers. They never spoke and kept to themselves. Gray and Carson began to give them names.

There was Grumpy, Dopey, Sneezy, Grumpy Two, Grumpy Three, and Kevin. Kevin was never in a good mood, and seemed to have allergies, but Grumpy and Sneezy were already taken.

At the end of the day, the pickers would deliver the crates to the warehouse workers, who would take them and load them on the trucks before sending them off into different directions, the fruit's destination to be a mystery to the rest of the men.

"Why do we never deliver to that warehouse?" Gray asked, pointing to the warehouse on the far end of the compound.

"No fruit there," the other man said in choppy English.

Gray let it go, but his curiosity was growing. They had been there for almost a month and had yet to deliver a crate to the third building.

The days passed by, and the boys continued to work. They talked with the other workers about the mountains, but were careful not to mention the treasure. Gray was afraid that one of them may try to find it for themselves. Carson was afraid that they would think that they were crazy. No matter the reason, the secret was safe.

******

It was late in the morning, and Gray and Carson were in the eastern fields picking blueberries. Gray was sneaking a few into his dry mouth when he saw Leila heading toward their room, carrying some lunch.

"There she is!" Gray said to Carson. "What day is it?"

"I think it's Monday. Tuesday? I don't know." Carson answered. It didn't matter. Gray was already off toward her.

Most days, lunch was delivered by Said's wife. It was always generous portions of fruits and falafel. Once in a while, though, Leila would deliver the food. Those were Gray's favorite days. He rushed toward the warehouse to catch her before she left.

Gray slowed down before he reached the door, took a quick moment to readjust his demeanor, then walked through the door, cool as a cucumber.

"Oh, hi," he said to Leila. "Didn't know you were here. What's on the menu today?"

"Hi, Gray!" Leila said. She smiled behind her mask. "Today we have some falafel. I made it myself. Try it."

She held out his plate. Gray took a bite and smiled back as he chewed.

"Himar yaemal with this falafel. Wow!" he said.

Leila's ears perked up, and she looked at him with bewilderment.

"What?" Gray asked.

"Did you just call me a donkey?" she asked.

Gray was dumbfounded. "No..," he began, "It means 'good job.' The others... they told me..." He realized that he had been fooled all this time.

Leila's laughter echoed through the empty warehouse. The embarrassment faded from Gray, and he joined in.

"Well, I should get back to the house," Leila said. "My father doesn't like me to be out here." She began to leave.

"Hey, wait!" Gray said. "Would you want to take a walk with me later? After I get done working?"

"Oh... I really don't think that would be a good idea," Leila said. "My father..."

"I understand," Gray said. "I could maybe talk to him. Let him know that I mean no harm?"

"No... he would kill you," Leila answered.

Gray laughed at that, but Leila's stone demeanor quieted him. He questioned whether or not she was serious.

"Well, if there's a way to not be killed and get to know you better, I would love that option," Gray said.

Leila thought about this for a moment. There was something deeper to Gray. She felt like she already knew him, but at the same time, may never know him at all. He was a mystery to her, disguised as an open book. None of it mattered, though. She knew that anything more than stolen glances would lead to nothing but trouble, maybe violence. Yet, something about him compelled her.

"Meet me in the northern fields tonight, after everyone goes to sleep," she said cautiously.

"I'll be there," Gray answered.

She walked out of the warehouse. Gray sat down at the table and stared at his falafel. *Amazing.* He held the fried patty under his nose and inhaled. *Leila.*

TWENTY-EIGHT

The sun had been set for a few hours and Gray was getting nervous. He waited around the warehouse for the rest of the crew to mosey off to their quarters for the night. There was an excitement in him that Carson could sense, but after the long workday, he was too tired to care.

The warehouse had finally quieted down, and Gray made his escape. After explaining what he was doing to his disapproving best friend, he climbed out of the window and followed whatever shadow he could find until he reached one of the furthest orchards.

The moon blanketed the ground with a soft blue light, lending itself to Gray's paranoia that he would be caught, castrated, and put on display for all the future farmhands to see. It reminded him of something his dad used to tell him. Beautiful women create bad decisions.

Every ounce of worry left him when he saw her. A movement in the distance, a silhouette of a woman, moving toward him with poise and confidence. Her face was no longer covered, and for the first time he saw her smile as she approached him.

"Hey," Gray said.

That was it. A love that would define them both began with one tiny word during a simple shared act of disobedience.

They walked together through the orchard, with the dark Atlas Mountains in the distance. Gray shared his travels and talked about his family. She talked about her time away at college and the wonders of the world. They laughed and shared and encouraged and teased.

The hour grew late, and they knew that they had to head back to their rooms. Gray walked with Leila as far as she would let him before turning him away before he could be seen.

Leila and Gray began to meet up like this almost every night. They would walk and talk about dreams and fears. Leila would speak about her dreams of leaving the farm, and her fears of her father. Her fears of an arranged marriage.

Gray would go on about his thirst for adventure and about the treasure and why they came to Ouarzazate. He told her about the drunken man in Cape Town.

It was the moments of silence, where they just held hands and walked, that spoke the loudest. They were falling in love with each other, and neither of them knew what to do with it. It bubbled up until one evening Gray turned to Leila to tell her how he felt. He stared into her eyes unsure of how to say it, until Leila kissed him.

They were both taken by the moment and fell into each other in waves. Their hearts gently twisted into one, and in so, they became indelibly woven into the fabric of one another. Together in Eden, Gray and Leila would love each other until the end.

******

The next morning, Gray woke up early and kicked Carson's bed, shaking him awake. Carson sprung to life from a dream, and took a moment to process what was going on.

"Morning!" Gray offered his groggy pal.

"What are you doing?" Carson said. "I was having a good dream." He laid back down on the bed. "I think… Dammit, I forgot it already."

"What are you talking about? Come on! The day is upon us. Destiny awaits!" Gray said.

"Oh yes, our destiny of picking berries and putting them into boxes. Can't wait to fulfill this destiny of ours," Carson said.

"Today is the day, my sarcastic friend. I'm going to talk with Said about taking some time off and heading into the mountains. We can't forget our purpose. The treasure is so close! We can't just stop now," Gray said.

He threw some pants at Carson and filled up a cup of coffee. The sun was just peaking over the horizon, and Gray was motivated like a boy in love.

They went to work under the hot sun. It was another day just like all the others had been. The men loaded up the boxes to send off to their random destinations, drank coffee, and exaggerated about the work that they had done.

After the day was over, rather than heading with the crew back to the warehouse, Gray went the opposite direction toward the house to talk with the boss. After their conversation, Said agreed to let him and Carson take some time off, but insisted on leaving some of their things to ensure their return. The deal felt strange to Gray. He began to feel like maybe he was more captive than employee.

He hurried back to the warehouse, eager to prepare for the trip to the Atlas Mountains. They were close to Mount Toubkal, maybe a two day walk, and Gray could feel the treasure out there, calling to him, just waiting to be discovered.

That night saw Gray and Leila's first fight. They sat in the grove as Gray told her about leaving in the morning.

"I'm in love with a fool!" Leila said to no one. It was darker than usual that night, as if even the moon knew to remain hidden behind the clouds, it too in fear of the woman's wrath.

"Oh, come on. Who's better at love than a fool?" Gray smiled, hoping to frame the argument in a more joyful way.

"You're not going to 'cute boy' you're way out of this," Leila said. "I can't believe you're leaving." She left a moment of silence to further illustrate her anger. "And how long will you be gone?" she asked.

"I already said... I don't know. As long as it takes," Gray answered.

"As long as it takes..," Leila said. She felt betrayed and used. "Just go then."

"I'm coming back, Leila," Gray said. "I have to do this. This is my purpose."

Leila sat in quiet, stubborn defiance. Her arms were crossed, and she was pouting like a child. Gray moved closer to her and put his arms around her.

"And when I do come back, I am going to ask your parents for your hand. I'm not going to let you be married off to someone else," Gray told her.

"My father will not allow that, Gray. He has his own plans for my future," Leila said.

"What does that mean?" Gray asked.

"We could just run away," Leila said, ignoring Gray's question. "We could take the horses, and be in Casablanca in a few…"

"I'm not going to just disrespect your family's culture," Gray interrupted. "I love you, Leila. When they see that they'll understand,"

"When my father sees that he will kill you," Leila said.

"Stop saying that," Gray said. "I mean it, I'll convince him. I promise."

"I mean it, too. My father is a very powerful man, but not a very nice man," Leila said. "There is more on this farm than berries."

Gray knew in his gut that something weird was been going on at the farm, but could never figure out just what it was.

"The other warehouse," he said. "What is in there?"

"Guns? Drugs? Your guess is as good as mine. I'm not allowed to go in there. But I know there's a lot of money coming from that warehouse, and it isn't from fruit," Leila said. "He's a dangerous man, Gray."

Gray looked at her. There was real fear in her eyes.

"Okay… Well then, let's do it," Gray said.

"What?" Leila said.

"When I come back from the mountains, you and I will run away together," Gray said.

TWENTY-NINE

Cool air reflected off the surface of the running water. Gray and Carson were following the river upstream toward its origin. The mountains in the distance were beginning to grow closer together, and Gray could feel the air getting thinner. Soon, the day would be over, and they would have to set up camp.

Carson dropped his bag and began to roll out their tent. Gray started a small fire. It was much easier now that there were trees around. And grass. Gray had a new found love for grass after his days in the desert.

"It's like we're in a whole new world," Carson mentioned.

The Atlas Mountains had life in all directions. There were fish in the river, and birds and badgers and gazelles in the woods.

"I love it," Gray said.

They had left most of their things back at the farm. Gray convinced Carson that it made more sense to make this trip on foot and packed light. He didn't want to bring up the possible prisoner situation back at the farm. Besides, the mountains wouldn't be kind to the camels. They would just have to worry about hauling their treasure back home once they found it.

They relaxed by the fire. The smoke floated off into the clear night above them. "Holy shit..," Carson said, "Look at that!" He pointed to a nearby tree. There was a large black owl staring back at them. Its orange eyes were shining through the dark.

"Do not trust the black owl..," Gray said.

"I gotta be honest here, I thought that drunk old man was just being needlessly cryptic..," Carson said.

"Just a coincidence," Gray said.

"Doesn't feel like one," Carson responded.

The owl left the branch and flew off into the night.

"See? He probably found a little rabbit or something. I'm gonna get some sleep," Gray said.

The morning came quickly and with it, a new challenge: the mountains. The river that they were following had morphed into a small stream as they got closer to the source. Gray was jumping over it back and forth and beginning to annoy Carson.

"Must be nice to be able to live life as one big easy joke," Carson said.

"What the hell does that mean?" Gray stopped jumping and walked with his friend.

"It means that I've been traversing through Africa for months on end. I've quit my job. I don't have any way to make a living, and I have nothing to show for it. All because of you and your *destiny*." Carson said.

"I thought you liked Africa?" Gray said. Carson could always be a little dramatic, but this felt different.

"I love Africa. I could actually see myself living here! You just don't understand. You and I don't get the same ride in life! You just don't get it, man. Life isn't some big fun game. It's sickness and sorrow and sweat and tears," Carson said.

"What are you talking about? Think of the experiences we've had!"

"Fuck experiences. I don't have a trust fund to go home to, Gray. This was the dumbest thing I could have done. Following you to God knows where, for some treasure that some drunken fool mentioned briefly... It's ridiculous. You're ridiculous. You're a man-child. I'm stuck working my ass off at some farm while you're out sneaking around with the boss's daughter," Carson said.

"Don't bring Leila into this," Gray said.

"She's the whole reason why I'm still stuck in Africa! We could have left months ago, but no. No. You were too busy with some girl," Carson said.

"I'm in love with her," Gray said. He stopped walking. Carson took a few more steps forward and turned around to face him.

"Oh god, you have got to be kidding me! You're in love with her? It's been what, two months? See? This is what I'm talking about. You're a child," Carson said. "What the hell do you know about love?"

"I just know it. It's like instinct or something," Gray said.

"You're ridiculous. I should go back. Maybe I can get my job back if I explain everything."

"Carson, listen to me," Gray began, "You're not going to need a job ever again once we find this treasure. Just give it a few more days!"

"A few more days? 'A few more days' is what I've heard for months!" Carson said.

"Okay, look," Gray said. "As soon as we get back to the farm, Leila and I, we are going to run away.

We will be back in Kenton before you know it, man. Just trust me a little bit longer."

"Were you not going to tell me about this? Were you planning on just leaving me behind too?!" Carson said.

"Of course not!" Gray said. "I figured the three of us could sneak off and make our way to Casablanca before anyone would know. We could hop on a ship from there. I don't know. I'm still trying to work out the details."

Carson couldn't take it anymore. He started kicking the stream at Gray, sending water flying all over him. Gray ducked under the onslaught and quickly fired back, soaking Carson. The two walked in damp silence.

"And I'm hungry!" Carson yelled into the surrounding forest.

They came upon a small footpath that led from the stream up through some rocks and deeper into the mountain. The two walked in single file through the woods until it opened up into a clearing. There was an enormous stone surrounded by a few small wooden shacks. From the looks of it, they had long since been abandoned. A black owl perched on the stone, staring down at the men.

They approached the stone. The owl flew away as they neared. It looked as though it had been carved by hand, but there were no markings on it. No decorations. It was as smooth as marble.

The afternoon was getting late, and dark clouds rumbled in the distance. A storm was on its way. Gray approached one of the small homes and gave a timid knock to the door. No one answered.

"Hello?" he yelled into the window. There was no one home.

He knocked on the door of the next house. Again, nothing. He looked back at Carson and shrugged before kicking the door open.

There wasn't much inside but a few beds, an empty bookshelf, and a small wooden table in the middle of the room. On the table, however, was a steaming bowl of pasta. Plates and silverware were waiting at the chairs. It was as if the meal had been prepared for guests. Carson gave little thought to the situation, rushed past Gray and began to dig in.

"We should wait out the storm here, I suppose," Gray said, "I'm guessing that whoever lives here will be back soon. We should probably save them some of the food?"

"Let's hope it's not a family of bears…" Carson said between bites.

The sky grew dark, and the storm arrived. Thunder and lightning fought across the sky. The sound of howls outside drew Gray's attention. He looked out the front window to see four large dogs near the stone. They were each sitting patiently, staring at the shack.

Gray was uncomfortable. This was all too weird for him. He liked easy. The dogs began to bark toward the house. He couldn't help but feel that they were calling to him. He opened the door and approached the animals. The dogs stood up and began to wag their tails as he slowly walked to them. They turned toward the woods, looking back at Gray. He stopped, hoping not to scare them away. Another dog began to nudge Gray from behind, pushing him forward.

"Where did you come from?" Gray asked the dog.

It nudged him forward once more before running ahead to join the others. They wanted him to follow.

"Okay, okay…" Gray said, "Let's go?"

The sky rumbled again as they made their way through the forest. The dogs kept near Gray while he climbed the steep pathway, leading him deeper into the mountain. Eventually they broke through the tree line, and Gray found himself at the edge of a huge gorge with a small lake at the bottom. On the far end of the gorge was a waterfall. The view took his breath away. It was another world. Without warning, the dogs darted back off into the woods, leaving Gray behind alone.

"Wait!" he called after the animals. A few drops of rain hit his shoulder.

There was a commotion in the woods. Gray stood still waiting, but was relieved to see Carson break through the tree line. He had been trailing them from the abandoned shack.

"Couldn't have let me know that you were going to go exploring the possibly haunted woods? Jesus, man… Another example of…" Carson was immediately silenced by the view before him. "Wow… This is incredible," he said.

"Those dogs led me here," Gray said.

"What dogs?" Carson asked.

Gray didn't know how to explain it, so he just turned back around and took in the view. Gray pointed to the waterfall.

"At the end of a deep gorge, beside a waterfall..," he said.

"But you cannot go there. Kaafir are not allowed… remember the last part?" Carson reminded him.

"What, are they gonna check our IDs? Come on!" Gray began toward the opposite side of the gorge. He was looking for a way down that didn't involve jumping eight hundred feet into a mysterious body of water at the base of a mysterious waterfall.

The sky rumbled again, and the rain finally came in sheets. Gray found a spot along the rocky wall that they could potentially climb down. He sat on the edge and maneuvered himself onto the face of the rocks, the rain making it slippery. The temperature was dropping fast, and it was getting colder.

Carson followed, carefully placing his foot on the jagged rocks. Lightning lit the sky up, and for a brief moment they could see the water churning below. Carson took hold of an overhanging rock but had trouble holding on. His hand slipped, and he began to lose balance. Gray reached out to help him, but the weight was too much and the two boys fell into the frigid water below.

The impact took Gray's breath away as he scrambled through the water, desperate to find the surface. He broke through the surface and called out for Carson, who broke the surface next to him, gasping for air. The heavy rain battled the senses. All Gray could hear was the downpour. All he could see was darkness. He couldn't tell which way was which. A quick blast of lightning illuminated the rocks near the waterfall. Gray could barely make out a dim light glowing from a small entrance in the rocks. He grabbed Carson, and the two began swimming toward the edge of the water.

The dark water rolled over them as they cut through toward the opening. Gray reached out to the rocky wall and began to climb. The opening was close, maybe twenty feet above them. The rain was punishing. The two were soaking wet and cold from the wind. Gray reached the opening first and rolled into the cave. He held out his arm to Carson and helped him out of the water and into the shelter.

A small bonfire was glowing toward the rear of the cave. The light flickering off of the walls illuminated the enormous area before them. Golden helmets and coins were hastily tossed around covering the floor. A family of jewels was left spilled onto the ground from an overturned chest. Random trinkets and treasures lined the walls. It was too much for them to carry. On the far side of the room, sat an empty throne, adorned with ornate carvings and diamonds. Green fabric covered the seat. It was a throne fit for a beautiful palace, not a dimly lit cavern.

"Jesus… we're rich!" Carson said. He couldn't believe his eyes. He immediately ran to the treasures and began to sift through the coins. Gray stood there flabbergasted. He was vindicated. The treasure was real. It felt good. It felt like destiny. He joined in with his friend.

"You'll never have to work again, buddy," Gray said.

Carson didn't hear him. He was singing an old show tune and dancing with an empty dress that was found in some old luggage. It looked like something a queen would have worn a thousand years ago.

Thunder rumbled outside, and Gray turned back to the entrance of the cave. The rain was still pummeling the earth outside. They would have to wait out the storm in the cave. They, however, were not alone. Something stood in the entrance watching them. A silhouette of an owl contrasted the gray clouds beyond. The fire danced in the reflection of its eyes.

"Carson...," Gray whispered.

Again, Carson didn't hear him. He was too busy wearing an old helmet and swinging a bronze sword.

"CARSON!" Gray yelled. Carson looked up, the helmet fell down over his eyes.

"What?" he asked as he took the helmet off and tossed it to a nearby pile of coins.

Gray nodded toward the owl. It gave them no reaction. It just stared back at them, its eyes piercing deeper into Gray each passing second. He felt as though there was something more there than a bird.

The fire began to roar behind the men, and they turned to see that their treasure had now vanished. Gray had a bad feeling in his gut.

Slowly, the figure began to change before them. It grew taller and wider and eventually into the shape of a man. Lightning flashed across the sky, showing his true form.

"Who!?" the man bellowed.

"Oh hell… He's still speaking owl!" Carson said.

"No I'm not! You didn't let me finish… Who the hell are you two fools?!" The man's voice boomed through the cavern..

"Oh, uh…," Carson said. "Sir, we are Americans. My name is Carson, and this is Gray. We are very sorry if…"

"What color is your soul?" the man asked.

"What?" Gray said.

"Red, white, and blue, baby!" Carson said.

"No! No…he's just kidding! Come on, dude," Gray interrupted.

"What color is your soul?" the man asked again.

Gray thought back to the old man in the market. *I had no green. I had no yellow.*

"Green…," he said.

"THANK YOU!" the man said. "No one EVER gets that right. I mean, come on! There are so many clues."

"That's it?" Gray asked.

"That's it," the man said. He walked toward the old throne and took a seat. The fire calmed back down and gave the cave a nice, relaxing glow. Gray could smell lilac. The man was wearing a long purple robe that swept the floor under his bare feet. He was enormous, easily seven feet tall and muscular. His long white beard contrasted with his dark, young eyes, making it difficult to guess his age.

"Who are you?" Gray asked again, walking slowly toward the man.

"My name..," the man said, "is Abu al-Walid Shamhurish, at Tayyar. I am the flyer. One of the Seven Kings of the Djinn…,"

"Djinn?" Carson asked.

"Like a genie?" Gray asked.

"No! No, no, no… not like a genie. We are so different!" Shamhuresh said.

"What's the difference?" Gray asked.

"There's so many differences. For one, genies aren't even real."

"Do you live in a lamp?" Carson asked.

"Ugh… Okay, I have lived in a lamp once, yes, but I only did it when I was between places! I wasn't like, forced into it or anything," the djinn said. "It was a super temporary situation."

"I don't know. Sounds kind of like a genie to me. Do you grant wishes?" Gray asked.

"I don't want to say…," Shamhurish said.

"You grant wishes! You're a genie!" Carson said.

"Okay, here's the thing…,"

"I knew it!" Gray said. He stepped closer to the djinn.

"Okay… I do grant wishes…" Shamhurish said. "But only because I want to! And you don't get three wishes, that's so dumb, and you can't wish for more wishes, obviously. There's no loophole in wishes. I only do it because I want to! I'm not a genie! I'm a king, dammit!"

"Sure, sure… That's cool. Not a genie. You just live in a lamp and grant wishes. I get it," Gray said.

"LIVED," Shamhurish corrected. "I told you, it was a temporary thing."

"Where do you live now?" Carson asked.

"Oh… yeah. Like I'm going to tell you guys where I live," Shamhurish said. "My privacy is important to me, okay?"

"Sure," Gray said, "So what does a djinn do as opposed to a genie?"

"I help people," Shamhurish answered.

"We don't need any help," Carson stated. "We just want our treasure, and we will be on our way, sir."

"You mean *my* treasure?" the djinn said as he stood from his throne. The fire began to roar again. "Absolutely not. You can't have it."

"Whoa, surely we can work out some kind of deal here?" Gray said, trying to cool things back down. "You just said that you help people, right? We don't want all of it, just some of it to *help* us out."

The storm continued to rage outside the cave's entrance. The wind beat against the walls. Shamhurish walked toward the entrance and looked out at the sky.

"You will get no treasure," he said. "But, to acknowledge the journey that you have taken to get here, you may each have one wish. Let's say that it's a consolation prize of sorts. You can take the night to think about it. In the morning, you will be on your way."

Beds appeared next to the back wall. A small feast was found on a long table near the other end. Candles flickered, and the light reflected off of a greasy cooked chicken. It was covered with rosemary and thyme. The men, who had mostly forgotten about their hunger until now, found themselves drooling at the sight of the food and wasted no moment before digging in. They agreed to stay, and began contemplating their wish.

After the meal, both Gray and Carson had no trouble falling asleep. They were exhausted from the day, and their bellies were full from djinn's feast.

The storm died during the night, and Carson woke up to the sounds of hushed voices. He rolled over and looked toward the entrance. The silhouettes of Gray and Shamhurish were cut by the moonlight. They were speaking quietly. Carson grew suspicious of his friend.

His jealousy was always there, under the surface, but now it seemed ready to boil over.

He's betraying me. He's going to wish for all of the treasure for himself. Or more! Like he needs anything. Everything he has, was given to him.

Gray thanked Shamhurish and made his way back to his bed. Carson rolled back over, pretending to still be sleeping. He gave a few fake snores to help sell the con.

The morning came, and the sun poked out through the forest beyond the waterfall. Birds began to chirp in the distance. Carson opened his eyes and snuck out of bed before Gray woke up. He approached the djinn, who was sitting at the entrance, facing the outside.

"You're up early," Shamhurish said.

"Early to bed, early to rise," Carson answered. "I've decided my wish."

"Treasure?" the djinn guessed.

"No. God, no. I'm tired of treasure hunting," Carson answered again.

"I can't give you love."

"Yeah, I know how the genie rules work," Carson said.

"I'm not a genie!" the djinn said.

"My wish..," Carson said. "I wish for you to ignore Gray's wish. Whatever he wished for, I want you to deny it."

Shamhurish raised his eyebrows at this. "You want me to deny his wish? Are you sure?" he asked.

"He has everything he could ever need and more. It's time he learns a lesson. He needs to learn what it's like to not get what he wants for a change," Carson said.

"Interesting," the djinn said as he stroked his long beard.

"Do we have an agreement?" Carson asked.

The djinn stood from his chair and shook his hand. "Your wish is my command," he said.

Carson nodded, and went back to the beds and picked up his clothes. The morning was rushing by, and they needed to get back to the farm. He kicked the bed that Gray was sleeping on, shaking him awake.

"Good morning, buddy," Gray said. He stretched and yawned.

"We need to get moving," Carson responded.

"Oh, yeah." Gray jumped out of bed and put on his pants. He looked for Shamhurish, but the djinn had vanished. There was no throne, no table, and no sign of any treasure. The cave was empty except for an old brass oil lamp sitting in the corner.

"I knew it," Gray said.

They two climbed out of the entrance and headed back toward the river, back toward the farm, and back to Leila.

THIRTY

It was night when they returned to the fruit farm. It had been nearly two weeks in the Atlas Mountains, and Gray was eager to see Leila. He had spent most of the nights lying in his cot, planning their escape, and he was certain he had all the details worked out. In two days, they would leave in the middle of the night. They would take two horses; one for Leila and Gray, and one for Carson, and the three of them would head northwest toward Casablanca. Once there, it would be easy to find a ship out of there, and maybe even one that was heading directly to the states.

Leila was nervous about leaving, but her mind was made up, and she was going to see it through. She wanted more out of life than the farm could offer, and she was determined to make her own destiny, and not be ruled by her father. There was trepidation in her decision, but ultimately she was in love with Gray. There was no other life for her, than one with him.

Gray and Carson entered their room and dropped their packs on the ground. It looked as though it hadn't been touched since they left. Carson shuffled off to his still unmade cot.

"Room service is kind of shoddy around this joint, eh?" Gray asked him.

"Yeah," Carson said.

"You alright? You've been quiet since the cave," Gray said.

"I'm just tired, Gray," Carson said. "I'm going to sleep."

"We will be out of here before you know it," Gray said, trying to boost his friend's morale. "Just two more days, then back to Kenton."

Carson offered no response, and turned his back to Gray. Gray shrugged it off and got ready for bed himself. He put on some clean shorts and got under his wool blanket. Sleep didn't come so easy that night. He was nervous about their plan, but eventually his worries threw in the towel, and his tired body won. He closed his eyes and dreamed of the river, of home.

The next morning when Gray woke up, Carson was nowhere to be found. Gray thought that maybe he was late to work, so he jumped into his clothes and rushed off to meet the crew.

The usual guys were still making their way to the fields, and Gray was relieved that he was on time for his shift. However, there was still no Carson. Gray worked through the morning, picking oranges while wondering where he could be.

Lunch arrived and Gray spotted his best friend walking toward the warehouse with Leila's mother as she delivered lunch. Gray made his way to them, thanked her for the food, and quickly asked Carson where he had been.

"What were you doing at the house?" Gray asked.

"Oh.., I guess Said heard that I used to work construction," Carson answered. "He is building a small barn and asked me to take a look at things."

"I see," Gray said.

After lunch, Carson joined back up with the crew in the fields. He was still quiet, but Gray chalked it up to their argument. He would just have to make it up to him when they got back to Kenton. He was sure it was nothing that a few beers together couldn't solve.

The next day, Gray got very little work done. He was nervous about their impending escape. Leila was about to give up her life in Morocco for one with him in Kenton, Illinois. She was trading a land full of wonder and magic for a river full of bait shops and chili cook-offs. There would be some culture shock. It was a lot to ask of someone. He felt the crushing pressure of commitment, and he knew that he had to make it worth it for her.

The work day was over, and Gray and Carson packed their things. They went through the usual motions. They had dinner and joked with the guys. Carson drank tea, and Gray read a book. They gave no hint of their plans of escape, but after the sun set and everyone had fallen asleep, they made their move.

Leila was waiting for them near the stable as planned. Gray let out a sigh of relief when he saw her. He wasn't completely sure that she would show.

They embraced before stealing two horses. They led them away slowly and quietly until they reached the end of the fields, sticking to the shadows from the mountains. At that point, Gray jumped into the saddle, helped Leila up, and they galloped off into the mountains. Carson followed behind.

The pale blue face of the moon was their only source of light through the dark trees. Gray felt an adrenaline the likes of which he had never experienced before. The only sounds were that of the horses breathing, and their hooves drumming over the land.

Carson was right behind them, and he, too, felt a rush. It wasn't the same romantic high of running away with the love of your life. He had a different kind of adrenaline coursing through his veins. It was something deeper; something more conflicted. His thoughts were interrupted by the sight of lights on the path ahead, and his silence over the last few days was broken.

"Up ahead," he said to Gray. They slowed their horses.

Gray recognized the men instantly. Grumpy Two was smoking a cigarette and holding a shotgun, looking off into the trees. Dopey and Kevin were arguing about something in hushed tones. They didn't seem to notice them yet. Sneezy, however, was staring right back at Gray. He yelled something in Arabic, and the others instantly turned their attention toward Gray and Leila.

"Shit!" Gray said. They bolted off the road and into the woods. Said's men jumped onto their horses and took chase after them.

"My father's men… How did they get ahead of us?" Leila asked Gray.

"I don't know," Gray answered. "It's like they were waiting for us!"

They continued through the trees and deeper into the mountains. The air grew colder. A gun shot rang out and echoed throughout the night. The men were firing warning shots into the sky.

A ravine appeared before them, and they slowed down for a moment to collect their bearings. Said's men were not far behind.

"We don't have many options here," Carson said.

"They're going to kill us..," Gray responded.

Another gun shot fired off in the distance.

"Leave me here," Leila said. "They just want me. You can get away. Leave me, and they will just take me home. They will kill you both!"

"I'm not leaving you," Gray said. "There's got to be a way."

"We should split up," Carson said. "They won't know who to chase."

"There's got to be another way," Gray said. He looked out into the ravine. There was no way down without breaking their necks.

"There's no other option," Carson said. "I'll get Leila to the city. You are the fastest. You can lead them away."

"No," Leila said. "We can't split up. That's crazy."

"He's right," Gray said. "You can double back and then make your way to the coast."

"No…" Leila said again.

"We don't have time to argue," Gray said. "I'll be fine. This is our best chance of not being killed. You and Carson head north and then double back. I can lead them away from here… It's our only option."

Carson moved his horse alongside them and helped Leila down from behind Gray. She reluctantly took his hand and climbed up behind him. Gray jumped down and loaded her gear onto the back of Carson's horse.

"Don't worry. This will work," Carson said.

"I'll lose them in the trees and try to meet you if I can. Whatever happens, don't wait for me. I'll see you in Kenton soon," Gray answered. "Thank you, Carson."

Carson snapped the reins, and he and Leila took off to the north. Gray jumped back on his horse and watched them as they disappeared into the dark mountains. He then waited until Said's men were visible.

"Hey himar lips!" he yelled at them. "This way you lazy bastards!"

The men gave him their attention, and Gray headed south. They followed after. Gray led them through a maze of trees and shrubs, with the sounds of hooves and gunshots echoing throughout the mountains. He rounded a corner and onto a path where he found a small inlet of rocks. It was just big enough for him to fit inside. He jumped off of his horse, grabbed his things, and gave the animal a smack on the backside, sending it off into the trees. The men came through shortly after and continued after the runaway horse. Gray had lost them.

He snuck away from his hiding place and stepped back out into the moonlight. The silhouette of the dark mountains stood beyond him. Gray knew that, on foot, he had no chance of catching up with Leila and Carson. No way to meet them in the city in time. He was on his own. There was only one thing left for him to do in Africa, and that was to find a way home.

THE VILLA LEILA

THIRTY-ONE

Theo drove across Maine Street with the windows down, letting the cold air from the AC mix with the waning humidity of southern Illinois in September. It was morning, and church was getting out. There were more bars than churches in this town, but not by much. He slowed down as an elderly gentleman pulled out of the parking lot at Saint Peter Catholic Church. Driving Lincolns in the Land of Lincoln.

He felt good today. He was in an upbeat mood, considering the recent events. After his divorce, Theo learned the importance of maintaining an emotional center. He tried meditation. He tried self-help books. But all he found from those were more and more self-help books. There was always another tactic, or another inspirational quote to read. He found himself so focused on who he wanted to be, he forgot to just be himself sometimes.

He drove by the fire department. His knee hurt. He missed his job. There was nothing more exhilarating than the pure adrenaline of moving through a fire. Voices through walkie-talkies. The heat. The intense, angry, angry heat.

The truck groaned to a halt as he pulled into the parking lot in the old downtown district. This had become a ritual for Theo. Before getting started on the day's project, he would come to this very coffeehouse and get his usual caramel latte. It was all the way across town from his father's house, but he would be damned if he was going to commit the same sins of his old man and settle for gas station joe.

He was waiting at the counter of the small shop when he heard the ringing of the doors. He turned around and saw her, the girl with the maple leaf tattoo. Her auburn hair curled at the ends. She gave him a friendly smile and got in line.

Do I buy her coffee? No, that would be too much. It would seem like a bribe. You don't want to have to bribe someone to like you, do you?

The steamer from the espresso machine raged like an old train engine. She approached the counter and ordered.

I should just be cool over here. I'll nod and leave. I'll just be cool. Keep her wondering. Be mysterious, Theo, you sexy pagan beast.

"Leo!" the barista shouted and placed a cup on the counter.

Theo moved toward the counter, "Did you say 'Theo?'" he asked.

"Leo!" the barista answered.

"Oh, no it's Theo," he laughed. "No biggie. Thanks!"

"No, it's LEO!" the barista said.

Theo reached for the coffee.

"HEY! That's mine! Get your meat hooks off it, pal!" a crusty old man said as he moved toward him.

"What?" Theo asked.

The old man poked him with his cane. "Get your hands off my macchiato, you bag of shit!" he said.

"I think there's a mistake here, sir. This is my order," Theo explained.

Maple Leaf had now joined the side of the counter, waiting on her order, watching things unfold. The old man poked him in the stomach again.

"Ouch!" Theo said. He held his hand out to fend off any future attacks.

"I've fought tougher pussies than you in Nicaragua. Socialist pussies!" the old man proclaimed.

"What the hell are you talking about?" Theo asked.

"I think he's talking about the contras," a bystander mentioned.

"Contras? What the hell?" Theo asked.

"Give me my coffee, punk!"

Theo held the coffee away from the man as he reached for it. "Stop it! This is my coffee you prickly old fuck!"

"No it isn't! You're a liar and a coward!" the old man answered.

"Reagan was an idiot!" Theo said.

The old man raised his cane again, and Theo grabbed it before he could poke him. "I'm gonna trickle down a beating on your socialist ass!" the old man declared.

"THEO," the barista yelled as he set another cup of coffee down. The cardboard cup made a loud pop on the counter top.

Theo stood frozen, with his hand still gripping the cane in the air. "Leo?" he asked the old man. The old man nodded yes.

"Oh… sorry about that. Uh… thank you for your service," Theo said. He let go of the cane and handed him his drink. The old man grumbled as he walked out of the shop.

Theo grabbed his order and thanked the barista who ignored him with ease. He turned to make his exit and found his only way out was past the girl.

"Hi," Theo said to Maple Leaf.

"Hi," she answered back through a small laugh.

"I don't normally fight geriatrics. Just when they step out of line," Theo said.

"I think he might have taken you," she said.

"He had a weapon!"

They shared a laugh. Theo reached out his hand. "We met briefly at the bar the other night," he said.

"Theo?" she said as shook it.

"How did you know that?" he asked.

She pointed to his latte. It read THEO in big black marker.

"Oh… right."

She turned her cup toward him so he could read the name.

"Al," he said, "Nice to meet you."

"Alexandria," she said. "No one wants to write that out all the time."

"I'd write that out. That's a beautiful name," he said. They shared a brief but comfortable silence.

"Well, I need to get going…," Theo said as they moved toward the door. "Hey, would you want to grab some coffee with me?"

"We're having coffee right now," she laughed again.

"Oh right, then a drink with me? When are you free?"

"Yeah. That could be fun. I'm free tomorrow." She smiled.

"Awesome." He held the door for her as they walked out of the coffee shop together. "I will see you tomorrow night at Cherry Street? Seven?"

"Sure, that sounds great," Al said.

HOLY SHIT, he thought. "Cool. See ya then," Theo said.

THIRTY-TWO

"I have a date tomorrow night," Theo said. He was sitting at the edge of the water in his father's secret fishing hole.

Mr. Jones was stalking a small frog. "Hell yeah!" he said, forgetting what he was doing and scaring the frog away. He had a bit of an attention problem. "Who's the lucky lady?" he asked.

"Her name is Al," Theo said.

The catfish floated on his back. He began spitting water out in spurts, resembling a shimmering little brown sprinkler. "What are you guys going to do?" he asked.

"We are just going to go get a few drinks," Theo answered. "Nothing too crazy."

"Drinks? No! You can't take this woman to get drinks. You need to romance her, man!" Mr. Jones said.

"What's wrong with drinks?" Theo said.

"It's boring. Love is supposed to be exciting! You gotta light a fire!"

Theo laughed. "I forgot, I forgot, you know everything about love. Okay, Mr. Jones, what do you think we should do?"

The fish pondered this for a brief moment. "Hmmmm..," Mr. Jones began, "Oh I know! You could go bungee jumping into a volcano!"

"That's Tom Hanks, man. That's Joe Versus the Volcano." Theo said.

"Right. Yeah, it's already been done… How about this? You take her horse-back riding into the sunset! Or wait, what about a long romantic walk through Madison Park in the fall? You could build a pile of leaves together and jump into it and fall in love!"

"I don't even have a horse. What are you talking about?" Theo said. "I can't do any of that. She'll think I'm a psychopath."

"WHAT?! The leaves are changing… It's incredible. That's romance, baby! Oh! You could meet on the top of the Empire State Building on Valentine's Day! Nah, that's probably been done. OR… WAIT I KNOW! How about this: a candle-lit picnic on the bluffs. It's a clear sky, and you've just shared a laugh… you catch each other's eyes and notice the glint of overwhelming desire and then when the time is right… BAM! You share your first kiss under the stars! A little bit of tongue…" the catfish said with a smile. "Make sure you have fresh breath! Here, breathe on me! I'll rate and review your kissing breath!" The catfish swam closer to the edge of the pond and offered his nose.

"I'm not going to breathe on you," Theo said.

"No?" Mr. Jones responded. "What are you hiding? You got a touch of the hal'?"

"I'll brush my teeth beforehand…," Theo said. "Anyway, drinks are a perfect first date and I'll tell you why. It loosens you up a little bit, helps with the nerves. It's perfect."

"Whatever you say," Mr. Jones said with the best shrug a catfish could give. "Not like I'm the master of love or anything."

"Besides, it's not like I'm staying in Kenton forever," Theo said, ignoring the sarcasm. "I'm just here to get this funeral over with. Then I'm going to heal up and get back to work. I can't fall in love right now."

"Then why even go on a date?" Mr. Jones asked.

"I don't know… I just kind of asked her, and she just kind of said yes. It was like instinct took over or something. I just went with it," he said.

Theo sat down on the bank. He felt good at this place. It was almost as if time stood still here. He needed to freeze time for a bit. Life was coming at him from every angle lately. "The funeral is coming up soon. It's in a few days," he mentioned to the catfish. Mr. Jones didn't respond. "I could put you in a big cooler and take you with?" Theo joked.

"I don't know if the other guests will appreciate my presence," Mr. Jones said.

"I really don't think there will be many other guests," Theo said. "Dad wasn't really the 'friends' kind of guy."

"What? Abner was hilarious! And a good swimmer. And a good father. He was crazy about you!"

"You know, sometimes I think we are talking about two completely different people," Theo said as he threw a blade of grass into the wind. There was so much he was trying to wrap his head around. His mother's apparent murder. His father's best friend was a catfish. Bad magic in the river? "Help me understand something," Theo said.

"What's that?"

"Well, for starters, what in the fresh hell is going on around here?" Theo asked. "Where did you come from? What are you, besides a slimy little love guru?"

"Beats me," Mr. Jones said. He swam around a little bit before popping his head back up. "Are you familiar with Villa Leila?" he asked, nodding toward the small castle on the bluffs above them.

"Sure. I guess so. The guy was a recluse. Lost his wife or something. Long time ago," Theo responded.

"Magic is wild, Theo. It has its own rules. Or maybe even no rules at all. No one understands it, but sometimes it just happens," Mr. Jones explained. "And one time, something very bad happened up there... but at that same exact moment, something very good happened right here." He motioned toward the apricot tree.

"Okay...," Theo said.

Mr. Jones continued, "And when the good happened, it created me, and when the bad happened, it created him... It's like we needed to balance each other out."

"Him? Him who?"

"The monster," Mr. Jones said.

"Right, the monster... Okay, go on," Theo scoffed.

"Theo, you're talking to a catfish."

"Good point. So there's a monster in the river?" Theo asked.

The catfish nodded.

"What does the monster want?" he asked.

"It doesn't want anything. It's just pure hatred, Theo. It wants to kill the most important thing in the world."

"What's that?"

"Love," Mr. Jones answered.

Theo stood up and walked toward the apricot tree. He held one of the fragile shoelaces. It had been weathered by time. "These are my mom's, aren't they?" Theo asked.

The catfish sighed. "It'd be easier to just show you, but I can't. I only have one trick left."

"You only have one trick left?" Theo asked.

"Yeah, I already used up my tricks. I only have one left," Mr. Jones said.

Theo let the shoelace hang from the branch and went back to the water's edge. "You already used your tricks? What kind of tricks? What did you do?" Theo asked.

"Well, I used one of them to understand the ending to LOST. Remember that show? It was so good!"

"It jumped the shark after season three," Theo said.

"What?? No way, it was soo good!"

"They were all dead? Come on. That's just lazy."

"No! You just don't get it. It was about the journey, not the destination!" Mr. Jones said.

"Wait, you watched LOST? How did you watch it?" Theo asked.

"Abner brought a TV out here for me," the catfish said.

"Oh…," Theo said. "What else?"

"I used to watch old reruns of Cheers. That's another fantastic show. There'll never be another," the catfish said.

"No, I meant with the tricks. What other tricks did you do?"

"OH! Right. Well, for my other trick, Abner and I got rid of the monster. See, the monster... I don't know why, but it had grown weak. So we came up with a plan and trapped it in the river, but now that Abner is dead... the monster is gone. It's on the loose! I don't understand it either. My guess is that your father was what was keeping the monster at bay. But it's back now. Somehow..." Mr. Jones said.

"And you only have one trick left," Theo said.

"I only have one trick left," Mr. Jones repeated.

"There's bad magic in this river."

"There's bad magic in this river, Theo."

THIRTY-THREE

The early nineties were grumbling through the speakers at Cherry Street Tavern. It was early enough in the night that the usual crumbs of society hadn't quite crumbled in yet. Theo was in an older blue collared shirt with his sleeves rolled up, hiding a mustard stain from twenty minutes earlier, and regretting packing so lightly. As shoddily dressed as he thought he may be, he was well over the dress code for the evening. A group of older gentlemen covered in waterfowl camouflage were wobbling out the door when Al walked in. Theo caught her eye and waved her over to the bar where he was ordering.

"Hey! Perfect timing! What would you like?" Theo asked her as she approached.

"Titos and Seven." She smiled and took a seat.

"Titos and Seven," Theo repeated to the bartender. The bartender slapped the bar with some you-got-it attitude and began mixing.

Theo sat down next to her and said hello. They clinked their glasses together and plugged in. There was some small talk about the day and the usual awkward laughs. It was fun and exciting and terrifying.

"First dates, huh?" Theo said. He wasn't much of a ladies' man in the past. He married Caroline when he was twenty-five, and since their divorce six years ago, he buried himself in his work. There were the occasional late night last calls, and a short roster of unavailable twenty-somethings, which worked well for Theo. Who wanted to be available after a divorce like his? Love wasn't in the cards for a guy like him. He had a daughter to raise and a father to bury. He wasn't even sure why he asked Alexandria out. It just felt right, and at the moment, he was very glad he did.

"Date?" she asked. "Who said anything about a first date?"

"You're right, this is our second date, I almost forgot about coffee yesterday!" Theo said.

Al laughed. "Okay, you're right. Well, then that one will go down as one of the weirdest first dates I've ever been on. I can't believe you made it to the second!"

"That's how I do it, I assert my dominance by picking fights with old war veterans."

The bar was full all around them, but they hardly noticed. They had another round and talked about dreams and family. They shared ghost stories from childhood. There was no talk about death, or divorce, or bills, or anxiety and dread. There was only laughter and focus. Al moved her leg across Theo's shin. Theo felt it in his stomach.

"Theo," Al said as she sat her drink down and grabbed his hands. "I've got a great question. What's your first memory?"

"My first memory?" Theo asked.

"Yeah, like the very earliest blur that comes to your mind?" Al said.

"Oh, that *is* a great question. Let me think... What's yours?"

"I can remember my mother in a rocking chair. I was walking toward her and she was singing. I don't know the song, but I remember the voice. I remember the light through the window... then blank," Al said. "Memories are strange. I don't know why I remember that moment and nothing else from then, but it stays with me. There was nothing special about it, but it is so full of joy that I think it's given me something."

"Given you what?" Theo asked.

Alexandria had spent the last eight years working her ass off building an oftentimes scoffed at art-therapy practice for children. She had to get her degree overseas because the states didn't even recognize it as a real discipline. She studied in London, and then did her graduate degree in Spain. Now she was back in Kenton, determined to help make a difference.

"Not sure. Maybe a purpose?" she answered.

"That's beautiful," Theo was a little buzzed.

"Fucking right it is," she said as she slammed the rest of her drink.

Theo straightened his back. "Wow, the first memory that I can summon from the depths of darkness in my brain... Well... I remember being little and laying on the floor looking at the ceiling fan. The television was on and my father was watching TV. I remember him standing up, and I rolled over... and then," Theo paused. "Hmm..."

"What?"

"And then my father came over and started to tickle me with his feet. I laughed like crazy, and then he picked me up and gave me a big hug before tossing me on my bed," Theo said.

"That's a nice memory," Al said.

"Yeah." Theo felt it.

They were interrupted at the bar by Huckleberry Gary. He had recently stumbled in for his usual game of pool. He smelled like a frat house. He landed on the bar next to Al and placed an empty bottle of beer on the bar.

"What's up, you two!?" he said.

"Hey Gary. How are you doing?" Theo asked.

"I'm fucking... awesome!" Huck responded. "Another one, please!"

The bartender brought a bottle of beer. Theo told her to put it on his tab. Huckleberry walked around and stood next to Theo. "Thanks, brother," he said to Theo with a fist bump.

"No prob, Gary," he said. "Gary, this is Alexandria."

"Al," she said as she shook his hand.

Huck looked at both of them. "Ohhh, I see. Meeting some of the locals before you head back to the big city?" he asked. There was an awkward silence. Al excused herself to use the restroom.

"I saw you the other night," Huck said. "You were driving out beneath the bluffs."

"No, I don't think so," Theo said. He didn't think there was any good way to explain that he was out hanging with his new friend, a talking catfish.

"Yeah, yeah, I did!" Huck slurred. "It was right out by the Star-lite. Did you hear about the murder?!"

"Murder? Who was killed?" Theo asked.

"Some doctor…. Doctor…. Oh, I know this. Dr. Anderson!" Huck said.

"Dr. Anderson?" Theo couldn't believe it. That was his father's doctor.

"Yeah, you know him?"

"Uh… yeah. Yeah, I did. I mean I do," Theo answered. "That was my dad's doctor."

"Interesting," Huck said.

"What's interesting?" Theo asked.

"Just a coincidence is all, you driving around so close to the time and place that your dad's doctor was killed," Huck asked again.

"That wasn't me," Theo insisted.

"Yes it was. I saw you!"

"Huck, I think you're mistaken, man." Theo had no idea how to begin explaining that he was visiting a magical catfish.

"Why are you lying to me?" Huck asked.

"I'm not lying," Theo said.

"Yes, you are. You're fucking lying to me. I saw you in a truck." Huckleberry was getting a little aggressive now. "Are you hiding something, Theo?"

"Okay, listen," Theo stood up from his bar and leaned closer hoping to deescalate the growing tension. "I was driving my father's truck around and was feeling kind of down about everything. I didn't want to say anything because I was embarrassed."

"What do you mean you were embarrassed?" Huck asked.

"Come on, man. I was crying, okay?" Theo said.

"There's no shame in a man shedding his tears, Theo," Huck said.

"Well, I just don't want anyone to know. Keep this between us?" Theo said.

Huck looked him in the eyes. They stared at each other for a minute. Theo was doing his best to sell the lie. Al rejoined them and sat back down.

"Huck! You're up!" One of the vets yelled from the pool table near the back door.

Huck clinked his bottle to Theo's. "Thanks for the beer," he said as he walked back to the pool table.

"Making friends again?" Al laughed.

Theo sat back down and laughed with her. "Apparently, I don't play well with others," he said. It was nearing midnight, and they decided to have one more round before paying the tab. "Well, it's getting late. Can I walk you home?" Theo asked.

"I suppose," Al said.

Theo opened the door for her, and Al stepped onto the sidewalk. Moths were circling the dim bulb that illuminated the old wooden bar sign. They headed down the sidewalk and walked and talked under a clear fall night in Middle America. Al grabbed Theo by the arm and held on tight. Theo flexed his arm but pretended not to. She knew what he was doing and laughed to herself. The air was clean, and the river was less than a mile away. They took a corner into an older neighborhood with a road still built with red bricks.

"What happened to your leg?" she asked.

"Fell off a ladder," Theo answered.

Al didn't know if he was joking so she just laughed. "So mysterious," she teased him. Theo laughed.

"It's kind of a long story," Theo said. "I'll tell you next time."

"Oh, next time? Bold of you to assume," Al said.

"Oh... there's gonna be a next time!" Theo responded.

They turned another corner and slowed down in front of a small house with the porch light on.

"This is me," Al said as they stopped. "I'm glad we did this. I had fun."

"I did too," Theo said. They caught eyes, and Theo felt himself no longer in control. Instinct once again took over. There was no other way to explain it. It was simple, pure instinct. He moved closer offering a kiss, and Alexandria accepted. There was a moment when the warmth of her lips hit his, and he forgot where he was. He was home again, but yet for the first time. They finished their embrace, and she smiled at him before walking away.

"Thanks for the memory," she said as she opened her front door. Theo smiled back. *Wow,* he thought.

There aren't many ways to describe it. How can you use the same word for something like a pair of jeans? It's the right note in the right song. Chills and sorrow because life is temporary. It's everything in the middle of nothing. Singularity. Instinct and luggage. A song that you'd be embarrassed to be caught listening to. It's a storm in the Midwest. A wave and a blinking eye and a late night and a cigarette and a June bug and a cold cup of coffee and a ceiling and a drunken conversation with God. Theo didn't want to let it in, but he couldn't help it. Who is brave enough to fall in love in Illinois?

He turned around and almost danced along the sidewalk. His head was in the Midwestern clouds. *Kiss her under the stars!* He thought of his catfish friend's dumb advice. He could almost kiss him, too! And for a brief moment, life made sense.

A block away under the shadow of an elm tree, stood Dino Perez. He had watched as Theo and his date laughed at the bar. He watched as they shared their first kiss. He had been following him all day. There was something going on in this town that Dino was going to get to the bottom of; and Theo Beckett was suspect number one.

THJRTY-FOUR

Twenty Minutes Earlier...

Huckleberry Gary was drunk and smoking the remains of an American Spirit that he had found on the ground. He was leaning against the dumpsters of the Cherry Street Tavern, contemplating taking a piss right then and there. It was nearing midnight, and the sounds of the small river town were blanketed by the muffled noise of the manufactured joy that can only be found in a local tavern.

People wear alcohol as a mask to their pain, Huckleberry thought to himself. He knew it went deeper than that. That lazy excuse was neither accurate nor profound. There's a maze that runs through every man's mind. Sometimes you just get lost.

Huck finished his smoke with one last greedy drag. The filter burnt his finger, and he tossed it to the ground, immediately realizing he was next to a dumpster. He picked it back up off the ground, lifted the lid, and tossed it inside.

Theo Beckett is hiding something, he thought. *What wasn't he telling me?* Huck knew that he saw him driving outside of that motel. There was no doubt in his mind. *Did he have something to do with the murder of that doctor? His dad's doctor. Maybe he blamed him for the death?* Huckleberry Gary, ever-burdened with the plight of the protector, knew he had to take action.

The door to the tavern opened, and Al stepped out and into the night. Theo followed, and they turned and walked down the sidewalk.

Huck waited until they were further down the way before following. He stuck to the shadows of the front yards and stayed off the sidewalk so as to not be seen. He was one with the night. He was the shadow. He probably should have peed before he left, though.

They took a corner up ahead, and Huck thought that maybe he saw another person across the street. It looked like an older man with a black fedora. *Could have been my imagination.* The light can play tricks when you're a few bottles in. Theo and his date stopped about a block ahead. Huck leaned behind a tree. The two just stood there for a moment before embracing. Huckleberry Gary scoffed to himself. He peeked out from his hiding spot.

The girl went inside her house. Theo skipped a few steps and then continued walking. Huck continued to pursue. Theo took another turn and walked into a park area. There were no street lights for a few blocks and without the perfect moonlight, it would have been hard to see anything. The sounds of a small creek that ran through the park came into earshot.

Huck couldn't handle the pressure anymore. Peeing was eminent. He walked a little deeper into the moonlit woods and found a tree to mark. The sweet relief gave the drunken servant of the people chills.

He came back to the sidewalk and found his target gone. There were no signs of Theo ahead. He quickened the pace and came to a fork in the road. On the right was a wooded path that went closer to the river and deeper into the woods. On the left was a sidewalk that led back into town and toward Theo's father's house. *Obviously he went left*, Huck thought; but the sounds of leaves crackling on his right changed his mind. He peered into the dark trees. A branch snapped. There was someone there.

Huck crouched back into the shadows and headed toward the sound. He was careful with his steps, and although drunk and wobbly, his adrenaline kept him tight. He pulled a combat knife from his waist and tiptoed through the trees.The sounds of movement came from his distant left. He stopped and ducked down lower. The creature moved through his line of sight quickly.

What the hell? Huck thought. He had a good look at it. The moonlight was reflecting off the creature's back. It had ragged, torn clothing and a long sharp blade fused to its hand. It turned its head. There was matted hair and nothing behind the eyes. They were cold and black. Dark moss covered skin reflected the moonlight, giving it almost a bluish hue.

"Theo?" Huck slurred.

The creature looked toward his direction. Huck panicked and hid behind a tree. He could feel the monster searching for him. He could feel it seething in the trees next to him. Huck gripped his knife, now scared sober. The monster moved behind the trees and headed further toward the river. Huckleberry Gary let out a sigh of relief and sat down on the ground to collect himself. The fear that pulsed through him had quickly become vindication. He had been right all along. He knew it!

Theo Beckett, you shape-shifting son of a bitch, Huck thought. *It's lizard season. Time to die.*

THIRTY-FIVE

Theo woke up on his father's couch feeling conflicted. He checked his phone. It was 7:30 in the morning. He pulled the curtains to let the light in. It was a beautiful morning after a beautiful evening.

He put some coffee on and looked around the house. Most things had been packed up and were in their final boxes. The mail had been piling up and was in stacks on the kitchen counter.

He couldn't help but feel guilty about his mood. He was in town for his father's funeral and yet, somehow, just had one of the best nights he'd had in a long time.

He took a quick shower and put on the black suit that he had packed for tomorrow's burial. He grabbed his coffee and a picture of his father and headed out the door. Theo stopped at the grocery store and bought a small bouquet of flowers before turning onto the highway and heading to Fall Creek.

******

Dino walked through the halls of the oncology department of the St. Thomas Regional Hospital. The harshness from the overhead panel lights were in complete contrast with the perfect autumn sunshine that was blessing the skies over Kenton. The smells of the sanitary wipes made Dino uneasy. He was in pretty good condition for his age, but it's never fun being in the hospital, healthy or not.

"What can I do for you?" a woman said from behind the reception desk.

"Hello," Dino said as he approached the desk. "I'm hoping to speak with someone about Dr. Ben Anderson? Is there anyone here who was particularly close with him?"

"Dr. Anderson is not here today," the woman said, barely looking up.

"Yes, I know," Dino said. "I was hoping to talk to talk to someone who was maybe close to him. Maybe a co-worker or someone?"

"We can't give that information out. HIPAA," she answered.

"HIPAA?" Dino asked.

The phone rang, and the receptionist picked up without a reaction. She seemed to be as equally invested in the phone call as she was with Dino's questions. *An unhelpful receptionist. Classic.*

Dino continued to wander the halls hoping to maybe find the good doctor's office. He was brushed past by a group of young doctors, following what seemed to be their mentor. They looked like a group of baby ducks waddling behind their mama. Dino could overhear the leader of the pack complaining to them. She mentioned her frustration in having to take on extra students this morning due to a Dr. Anderson's absence. Dino's ears perked up. He waited until the young medical students dispersed, clipboards in hands and lack of sleep in their eyes.

"Hi," Dino said to the frustrated doctor. "I couldn't help but overhear... You had to take on Dr. Anderson's students this morning?"

"I'm sorry," the doctor said. "Do you work here?"

"No," Dino answered. "No... I'm... I'm a detective."

The doctors left her notes to finally look up at the old man. "Oh?" she said. "How can I help you?"

"I'm looking for some information on Dr. Anderson, anything about his personal life maybe, that could help me out. Was he happy? Any enemies?" Dino asked. "Were you two friendly?"

"Friendly? No," she said. "No we are not. Not after today especially. I do not have the time to take on extra students. He and his floozy probably ran off together. They make me sick."

"His floozy?" Dino asked.

"Everyone knows about it. I'm sick of pretending it's not happening. He and Dr. Prynne. It's a little too convenient that they both missed their shifts today."

"That's a little extreme isn't it?" Dino asked. "I sincerely doubt that two doctors would just up and abandon their patients and job."

"Love makes you do crazy things," the doctor said. "Made me marry an absolute nightmare of a man. Forty-six years old, doing whippets and playing Fortnight... Ridiculous."

"Love?" Dino asked.

"Not anymore, it's been a rocky marriage for a while. Ebb and flow. I suppose that's life, though."

"I mean Dr. Prynne and Dr. Anderson," Dino said.

"Oh, those two are so gross. They think they are so smooth and secretive. Everyone knows that they are head over heels. They're probably making out next to some dumpster right now," the doctor said.

"Unfortunately, I doubt that," Dino said. "Dr. Anderson was found dead early this morning.

"Oh..," she said. She took a moment to gather her thoughts. "His wife did it. It was only a matter of time. I knew this was going to happen."

"No... I don't think so," Dino answered.

"Maybe it was her husband?"

"No... I'm pretty sure it was something else."

******

Theo made his way over the bridge and through the trees to find the pond as still as glass. He walked to the water's edge and placed the flowers and picture of his father on the ground near the tree.

"Hello?" he yelled at the water. There was no response. Theo sighed to himself, got down on his knees and stuck his face in the water. "Anyone seen a strange catfish?" he gurgled into the water.

Theo lifted his face to find Mr. Jones already at the surface, inches from him. Mr. Jones kissed him on the cheek. "Good morning, darling," he said, leaving a stream of catfish slime as he fluttered his eyes.

"GAH! NASTY!" Theo pulled away from the water and wiped his cheeks with some leaves so as to not sully his nice black suit.

"You look nice this morning," Mr. Jones said. "Quite toothsome. What's the occaysh?

Theo took a sip of his coffee and thought that maybe he didn't bring enough. "Well," he began, "The 'occaysh' is that I thought, you know, since you couldn't come to the funeral and all... I don't know, I thought maybe we could have our own funeral here."

The catfish swam to the edge and looked at the flowers and the picture. "I've never been to a funeral," he said.

"They're tons of fun," Theo said.

"Really?"

"No."

"What do we do?" Mr. Jones asked.

"I guess we should say some words. Maybe light a candle?" Theo said.

"Did you bring a candle?"

"No."

"Okay, well we can say some words. What do you have to say, Theo?" Mr. Jones said.

Theo thought for a moment. He didn't have much to say. "Well, I wish that Dad and I were closer," Theo said. "He was always very distant and wasn't very affectionate. It was a lonely childhood, and uh... I wish it was different. I'm thankful that I learned a lot of lessons in what not to do as a father, myself. I don't have much else to say... I mainly did this for Mr. Jones... my new catfish friend."

"Hmmm..," Mr. Jones said. He had a look of disapproval in his dark eyes.

"What?" Theo asked.

"Is that what you're going to say tomorrow?"

"I probably won't bring up a talking catfish."

"Okay. Maybe we say a poem or something?" Mr. Jones said.

Theo laughed at the notion. "A poem? I don't think Dad was one for the finer arts," he said.

"What? Are you kidding?" Mr. Jones said. "He loved poems!"

"Abner Beckett, my father, loved poetry?" Theo asked. He couldn't believe what he was hearing.

"Yep."

"He didn't even like knock-knock jokes," Theo said.

"He liked Whitman," Mr. Jones answered.

"You're kidding me," Theo said.

"The sun bursts through in unlooked-for directions. Strong thoughts fill you, and confidence... you smile!" The catfish continued, "You forget you are sick, as I forget you are sick. You do not see the medicines... You do not mind the weeping friends... I am with you."

Theo sat quietly on the edge of the water. He was jealous, sad, and angry. Why would his father keep so much at bay? Why wouldn't he just let him in? "I don't understand it," Theo said. "Why would he give so much of himself to you, and leave me with so little?"

"It's not that simple," Mr. Jones said.

"Did he blame me for my mother's death? I always thought that maybe that was the deal, but now I'm learning that even those details were kept from me."

"Theo," Mr. Jones said as he swam closer. "You have to understand that Abner loved you more than anything, but he knew that the only way to keep you safe, to protect you, was to hide that love away."

"That doesn't make any sense." They were interrupted by a ringing phone. Theo reached into his pocket and answered. It was Saylor on the other end. He answered it and spoke to her for a moment. "Okay, kiddo. See ya soon," Theo said before ending the call.

"Shoot, I'm running late," Theo said as he put his phone back in his pocket. "I have to go pick up my daughter. Her mother is meeting me halfway from the city. If she has to wait on me for even a few minutes, it'll be two days of texting, and I don't think I have the energy for that in me." Theo stood up from the bank of the water. "Let's put a pin in this. This conversation isn't over."

THIRTY-SIX

Caroline was filling up her blue Honda with gasoline. Theo pulled into the gas station where they had planned to meet and parked near the back of the building next to the air compressor.

"Hi Dad!" Saylor yelled from the back seat of her mother's car.

"Hello, Offspring!" Theo waved and walked to the car to let her out. He grabbed her bag and opened her door to let her out. The two of them walked to the truck. Caroline returned the gas pump to its resting place and followed them. Theo opened the passenger door to his truck and helped Saylor into the cab. Caroline's face remained stone as she stood a few feet away. Theo could see the resemblance of his daughter in her face. He found it to be funny.

It was a marriage destined to fail. The two met just after Theo got out of the fire academy. Caroline had just dropped out of school and was hoping to find herself. She took a job as a waitress, and the two hit it off instantly. They were in love within minutes. Dumb love always moves quickly, like a fire.

After a few months of dating, they talked about moving in with each other. The talking quickly turned to action, and before Theo knew it, they were sharing a one bedroom apartment in an almost-quiet suburb of Chicago.

Then one fateful evening after a twenty-four hour shift, Theo came home with a bottle of rum. He poured a drink for Caroline and then one for himself. He walked into the living room and offered her the glass. She started crying.

"I'm preggers," she sniffled through the tears.

Theo stood there, dumbstruck, not quite young enough to claim he was still a kid, not quite old enough to be ready to raise one. "Well...," he said before slamming both cocktails. "Fuck my face."

Saylor was born as healthy as a baby could be, and in an instant they both loved her madly. For one another, however, things would never be the same. Caroline was no longer the carefree spirit that she once was, and quickly became miserly with her love for Theo. Theo remained evergreen as a dreamer and expected a family that no one actually ever finds. They both began to blame each other for not having the life they thought they were supposed to have. The life behind a white picket fence. The divorce drew out the worst in them, and for two people that at one time loved each other without limits, they soon became embittered foes.

"When are you coming back?" Caroline asked Theo.

"The funeral is tomorrow. I have a few more things to take care of with the house. I don't have a specific day that I'm coming back yet," Theo said.

"I don't want Saylor missing that much school."

"She's in the fourth grade. I don't think it's that big of a deal."

"What does that teach her? I don't want her to grow up thinking that school is just something you can blow off," Caroline said.

"Okay, okay… I'll bring her back on Tuesday," Theo offered.

"When are you going back to work?" she asked.

"I'm not sure. The doc wants me to get back to physical therapy as soon as I come back to the city. She thinks it'll be a few months still."

"If we're going to co-parent efficiently, you have to keep me in the loop. I need to know your plan."

"I… I don't have a plan. I'm just taking everything day by day," Theo said.

"Typical."

"I'll have Saylor call you tomorrow."

"It's a two hour drive. Please have her home at a decent hour on Tuesday. What time can I expect her?" Caroline asked.

"Umm… I don't know," Theo said. "We will leave here at five-thirty and get to you before eight?"

"Fine," Caroline said. She walked away without saying goodbye.

Theo felt his body loosen up as she left. He hopped in the truck and turned the keys. Saylor noticed his posture.

"Whaddya think?" he said as he looked over to his daughter, hoping to reset the moment.

"Bowie?" she replied.

"Good call. That's my girl," Theo said as he plugged in his phone to the car stereo.

THIRTY-SEVEN

The funeral home was musty and quiet. Theo blamed the carpet. *They do this on purpose.* Theo thought. *They buy the thick carpet so it dampens the noise.* Why would anyone put someone who is on the emotional edge and the verge of tears into a giant sound booth? He decided then that there would be a DJ at his funeral. Silence is rarely helpful.

Theo stood at the entrance and greeted some of his father's old drinking buddies. There wasn't much of a showing for the family. There wasn't really much family to show. Abner was an only child, which was rare for his generation. Saylor was running around with Theo's cousin's younger cousin from his mother's side. He didn't know them well at all. Saylor was having some fun though. The laughter was in stark contrast to the quiet of the room.

It was in an old church Theo and his father used to attend long ago. The carpet was a deep red and made no noise even when walked upon. There were a few lines of candles in a recession in the wall. Theo remembered being a child and blowing them out one Sunday morning after Mass had let out. The priest clapped loudly at Theo and scolded him in front of his classmates. It terrified him. He was certain that he was going to Hell. An eight-year-old convinced he was going to burn for eternity; maybe that's why he became a firefighter.

Heather and Suzi greeted Theo with hugs. They were both dressed in black. Suzi looked out of place. Heather's closet was made for these moments. "Tough day," Suzi said as she slipped something into Theo's jacket pocket. The two made their way to the pews.

Theo reached into his pocket and found a tiny bottle of peppermint schnapps. A smile snuck up on him. He felt better having them there.

The liturgy began, and the few remaining people found their way to the pews. The priest said a few words, like he had said a hundred times before, wearing the same black cassock.

Theo had declined when asked earlier if he wanted to share anything. He didn't have much to say, and he still felt a tinge of guilt for holding on to some of his anger toward his late father. Theo stood behind the podium and looked out at the few members of the congregation. He wasn't sure what to say but he began anyway.

"I wasn't going to speak today, mainly because I had no idea of what to say until now. Well...I still don't really know what to say." Theo paused for a moment. "My father and I weren't as close as I wish we were. In fact, we weren't close at all, ever. It was a lonely way to grow up, and Kenton was a lonely town to grow up in. In fact, I always said to myself when I left, that I would never come back." Theo looked around the room and saw Saylor watching him. She was listening intently. Theo felt something. Instinct.

"However, now that I'm a father myself, maybe I get it. Maybe he was just doing the best that he could in the situation that he was in. I was recently talking with someone about memories. It's funny how some memories stick with you and can be so vivid and seem to almost take up the entire space in your mind. The oldest memory I have is of me laying on the floor and my father walking over to me. I was just a little guy, maybe six years old, and he walked over to me, and began to tickle me with his feet. I remember laughing so loudly that it bounced throughout the house. Then he picked me up and gave me a hug and tucked me into bed," Theo said.

He felt a lump in his throat. He couldn't figure out if it was longing or forgiveness. "My father loved Walt Whitman. I don't know much Whitman except for a small passage that a friend of mine gave me... 'You forget you are sick, as I forget you are sick. You do not see the medicines... You do not mind the weeping friends... I am with you.'" Theo stood there in wonder. The situation was catching up to him. "So... uh... rest easy, Dad. Thank you all for coming."

Theo walked away from the podium as everyone stood up to leave. Heather and Suzi met Theo at his chair with a hug. Saylor joined in on it.

"You may now leave in peace!" the priest dashed to the podium as the audience ignored him on their way out. The few that remained followed the slow parade to the gravesite where Theo stood like a statue as they lowered the dark cherry wood casket that held Abner Beckett into the ground.

THIRTY-EIGHT

Mi Queso Es Su Queso was the gold standard when it came to Mexican restaurants in Kenton. It had the regulation décor of piñatas, cacti, and an unintentionally-creepy stuffed monkey donning a sombrero while standing watchfully in the corner. Nightmare fuel for the children.

The lights were dim, and Heather, Suzi, and Theo were sharing a pitcher of margaritas. An ancient Pac-Man arcade game was clinging to its life as Saylor beat the two plastic buttons like they owed her money. It was dinner time and the group had decided to blow off some steam after the funeral. Cheese dip and margaritas are always in season for occasions such as these.

Al walked in and joined them. Theo poured her a glass and smiled. The salt slowly dissolved along the edge of the glass where the margarita spilled over. Al quickly lapped it up like it was a melting ice cream cone as Theo introduced her to Heather and Suzi. Saylor approached the table. "Dad, can I have some more quarters?" she asked.

"What am I? Jeff Bezos?" he shot back at her.

"Dad. Please?" she said.

"I don't know...," Theo said.

Saylor turned toward Al. "Did you know that this morning my dad farted louder than any fart I've ever heard before? It was the loudest fart in the world. It was the King of the Farts."

"OKAY! OKAY!" Theo interrupted her as he dug into his pocket and grabbed some change. She thanked him and went back to the machine. The table laughed.

"Oh, she's good," Al said.

"Yeah..," Theo answered. They raised their glasses and said cheers.

"Theo," Suzi said. "I thought today was beautiful."

"Yeah," Heather agreed. "Who told you that your dad was a Whitman fan?"

"Just an old friend of his," Theo said.

"Oh, I thought maybe your catfish friend mentioned it," Heather said.

"Catfish friend?" Al asked.

"She's just being weird. I'd say you'll get used to it, but you never will." Theo shrugged it off as he kicked his best friend under the table.

The restaurant was bustling. An old saloon door swung loosely as their waitress entered from the kitchen toward their table. "Well maybe if you spent your goddamn money on some proper shoes instead of all those goddamn swords, you wouldn't be slipping at the dish pit!" she yelled into the kitchen behind her before transforming into a smiling bundle of joy at the table. "How y'all doing?? Can I take these?" She motioned toward the empty plates. Theo helped her stack the dishes.

"So…what are everyone's plans for the rest of the evening?" Al asked the table.

"We're probably going to go eat some crab legs and take a bunch of Adderall," Heather said.

"NO, we are not," Suzi directed at Heather. "WE are going to be healthy and take a sunset hike." Heather rolled her eyes at the notion, before winking at Saylor.

"I'm just gonna get Saylor back to the house," Theo said before turning to Al. "What are you doing? Want to cook dinner with us?"

"I have plans tonight," Al answered. "But I'm free tomorrow night? Rain check?"

"It's a plan," Theo answered as he signed his credit card receipt. Saylor snagged an extra mint on the way out.

They said their goodbyes and parted ways in the parking lot. Theo led Saylor to his truck. The sun was setting into the early evening, and he was ready to put the day behind him.

******

Heather and Suzi hopped into Heather's little green hatchback and drove away. Suzi reached over and held Heather's hand as she looked out the window. "Let's take a little walk by the water?" she said.

"You want to go find a place to neck?" Heather asked.

"Maybe," Suzi said with a giggle.

THIRTY-NINE

Heather's little green hatchback zipped into the empty parking lot of an old a boat landing. The landing had been around for years and was in a sad state of decay. The old concrete was slowly crumbling into the muddy water of the Mississippi River. The years of drunken river rats pushing and pulling their boat trailers over it had taken its toll. There were ancient pieces of rope in the grass next to it. Beer cans from generations ago were still buried in the sand just below the water's surface. On the far end of the parking lot was the beginning of a hiking trail. It led along the water's surface through Dougal State Park.

"We used to come here all the time. Why did we stop?" Suzi said.

"Beats me. I guess life just gets in the way sometimes, huh?" Heather said.

The two walked together as the moon came out. It looked like an orange slice through the trees. Heather looked over and smiled at her fiancé. The two of them had never been more in love; the right kind of love. They were two people trying to be better versions of themselves, together.

"Oh my gosh!" Suzi began, "I forgot to tell you about my dream the other night."

"Oh?" Heather said.

"Yeah. It was the weirdest dream! You and I were hanging out and everything was pretty normal, but then I had to go to work... for some reason I worked at a Chili's Too... like in the airports."

"Which airport?" Heather asked.

"That doesn't matter," Suzi said.

"It does to me, but go on."

"So I'm late for work at Chili's Too, but I couldn't find my shoes. I'm looking all over for my shoes and starting to panic, and then my boss calls YOU to ask where I am. You couldn't think of an excuse, so you just told them that I was stuck in Hannibal for a dance contest. So then, I had to learn how to dance before I went to work so I could prove it to my boss. Luckily, I am an incredible dancer."

"You're a terrible dancer!" Heather said.

"I'm an incredible dancer, and you're a terrible liar!"

"You're right, babe," Heather said. "That's a crazy dream. I will meditate on the meaning for you. I had a dream the other night that I was in a dark swirling pit of despair. There was an evil fox running in circles, and the whole world was crumbling into deep, fiery gorges. The light of the world was slowly dimming as we all strolled one by one into oblivion. It was so peaceful... I haven't slept that well since I was a baby."

They walked on through the quiet woods. They held hands and talked about their wedding day and made plans for their honeymoon. Heather sparked a joint. The frogs began their regular evening set. Their croaks mixed with the laughter, and the world was good.

They came to a clearing from the trees and stepped out and then onto a small bank. The water was only a few feet away. The orange moon reflected off its surface in quick orange ripples.

There was a flicker of light from a large splash to their left. "That's a big fish," Suzi said, not realizing that it was no fish at all. It was something far worse.

The surface of the water broke, and the two looked in disbelief as the figure of a man emerged. It was as if he was walking up from the bottom of the river. There was no life in the creature's eyes, and he made no hesitation in approaching the women. The blade of an old rusted knife was fused to his hand and the two acted as one. The creature was stronger now. Its limp was all but gone.

Heather grabbed Suzi by the arm and pulled her out of paralysis.

"We need to get out of here!" she burst out. The two hit the woods fast, but the creature hit the woods faster. He cut through the trees and slammed into the women from the side. Heather tumbled to the ground, smacking her head against a tree. She could taste the blood from a cut on her forehead. It was disorienting. She was in a fog. The world was spinning. There was no up or down.

"Suzi!" she cried out to no answer. She made her way to her feet. There was the cracking of sticks behind her.

"Heather!" It was Suzi's voice. Heather ran toward the screams, still dizzy. A hand grabbed her and pulled her down into the dirt behind a fallen moss covered log. It was Suzi. *Oh, thank God*, Heather thought.

Suzi motioned toward the other side of their respite. The monster was just standing there looking around.

"Listen to me," Heather said. "We need to split up. I'm going to distract him, and you run."

"No, we can both make it! Are you crazy?" Suzi argued. The creature turned and faced them. It began toward the log.

"We don't have time," Heather said.

"We should have just eaten crab legs and took some Adderall." Suzi tried to remain upbeat.

Heather kissed her, and before Suzi could stop her she stepped out from the log and flanked the monster. It turned and pursued her, leaving Suzi at the log, speechless. Heather tried to maneuver through the trees, but the creature broke through them effortlessly. It was on her within seconds. It grabbed her by the back of her shirt and held her by the neck. She was spun around and faced the monster. Its glassy eyes were fixed on hers. She leered back into them in terror. There was nothing there but her reflection. The monster's eyes were just cold and black and full of hatred.

Heather tried to scream, but nothing could come to her mouth. She looked at the face just inches from hers. He smelled like old fish and mud. His tattered clothes were colorless, blending into his gray skin. What was once sandy colored hair was now matted and mixed with moss and dirt. From a distance, Suzi watched the monster hold her fiancé by the neck. "No!" She panicked and screamed. She couldn't bring herself to run away and had followed after.

Heather could only look at her. The monster saw the movement in her eyes. He threw her to the ground, and she gasped upon impact, confused and thankful to be alive. She felt pain flow through her arm in waves. Something was broken. She had no time to figure out what. She didn't understand. *Why did he stop?*

The river monster breathed in heavily. He turned away from Heather and toward Suzi. He had found his new prey and left Heather laying there confused. He was on Suzi before she could realize what was happening. She fell to the ground. The monster flipped her on to her back, held the rusted blade up, and stabbed her through the heart. Suzi gasped and then lay silent.

"No," Heather mouthed. Her voice was raspy and weak. Nothing made sense. There was panic and fear and confusion. The monster left Suzi's body and walked right past Heather barely giving her any notice before disappearing into the woods.

Heather ran to fiancé and dropped to her knees at her side. She held her in her arms, weeping and alone in the woods. Suzi, the single great love of her life, was dead.

FORTY

"Waffles," Saylor said without looking up from her tablet. She was watching instructional videos on YouTube on make-it-yourself slime. All she needed was shampoo, cornstarch, and a handshake from Satan himself, as she brought this kind of hellish substance to life.

"Waffles? No. We have apples. We have eggs. We have toast?" Theo responded, "Doesn't that sound good? Delicious and nutritious."

"Dad… nothing nutritious is also delicious. Come on. Let's do waffles. You deserve it. You've had a tough week. Come on, man," she bargained.

Theo was looking through the half-empty cabinets of his late father's home. The morning sun was shining through the windows. It was a new day, and Theo was enjoying breakfast with his car salesman of a daughter. "I sincerely doubt your grandpa had a waffle iron, kid," Theo said, looking behind the pots and pans.

"Pancakes?"

Theo didn't answer as he looked through the blinds of the window. Suzi's car sat in Heather's driveway alone.

"What are you doing?" Saylor asked from the kitchen.

"Being a nosey neighbor, what are you doing?"

"Being a nosey daughter."

Theo put on some music and got out the pancake mix. He looked at his daughter again. She was focused on her tablet. Pain shot through his knee, and he thought about the last fire call he was on.

******

It was an early morning in January, the first week of the year. The snow was black from the Chicago traffic, and peppered the streets around the firehouse. The cold bit your skin, and the sky was dead and gray, the heart of winter barely beating.

Theo reached into one of the cupboards in the shared kitchen and pulled out his secret coffee stash from behind a broken slow cooker. This was his usual hiding spot for some fine quality dark roast. He never understood the competitive nature between men and their love for terrible coffee.

The maker gurgled to life, and Theo looked out through the firehouse kitchen window. Some of the other firefighters were waking up and getting ready for the day. The B shift was a rowdy bunch of guys. Theo had been with the crew for eight years and knew almost everything about every one of them. They were thick as thieves, the B shift.

Theo poured himself a cup of coffee, but before he could take a sip the alarms went off. They always seemed louder in the morning.

The crew hustled to their lockers and stepped into their turnouts like they had done hundreds of times before. It took Theo a while to learn to roll his turnouts over his boots, so he could just step into them with one motion, but over the years, he had become just as quick as anybody. His gloves smelled like oil as he slid them over his hands.

The engine fired up, and they hit the streets with the siren blaring. An air horn lit up the neighborhood as it took the turn and headed toward the call.

It was an older apartment complex. The wiring in these buildings was never up to code. That's what frustrated the crew about so many fires. They were so avoidable.

Theo's buddy, Dan, was in the driver seat. He let out a sigh as he pulled to the side of the road and jumped out to work the pump on the top of the truck. Theo pulled a green tag from a Velcro patch on his helmet and handed it to the captain. The captain put it on a clipboard that he used to keep track of who was going to go inside, and who was going to stay outside to vent the windows and put up the ladders. Theo and his close friend, John, were going interior to make sure that there was no one left in the building.

The smoke was already heavy as the crew searched the building, knocking door to door to make sure each apartment was evacuated. Theo and John were climbing the stairs, complaining about every step.

"How can anyone still be in here?" John said, breathing heavily up the couple flights. Theo didn't respond. They both knew the answer. There was a problem with opiates everywhere, but this side of town especially. Over the years, Theo had found a number of people sleeping on their couch in the middle of a fire, unaware of just how tenuously their lives hung in the balance.

"Fifth floor," Theo said as they reached the top. "Welcome to the penthouse, baby."

John approached the first door and gave it a heavy knock.

"Fire Department!" he yelled into the wood. There was no response. He took his haligan and pried into the door jam, breaking it open. The two of them searched the dirty apartment but found no one. They were interrupted by a loud explosion below them. The ground shook for a quick moment.

"That's not good," John said.

They hustled into the hallway and on to the next door. Theo beat on the door hard. He ignored identifying themselves and got out his haligan to pry it open. Before he could, though, a man in his pajamas unlocked it slowly. He looked disheveled and completely out of it. "What is going on?" he asked.

"Party downstairs," Theo said. "Come on." He led the man into the hallway and was guiding him to the stairs when another explosion rumbled below them. Their walkie talkies came to life.

"THEO!" the chief said through the static. "Get out of there now!"

"There are three more doors!" Theo yelled back into the walkie talkie.

"Theo, we need to go! This floor is going to give out!" John yelled to him over the roar of the flames. The man in the pajamas was already running away.

"SHIT!" John said.

"Go! Get him out of here! I'll be right behind you!" Theo yelled.

"There is no time! Let's go!" John answered him.

"GO!"

John was visibly annoyed. He had no choice but to follow the man and get him out of there.

"Goddammit, Theo," he said as he ran to the stairs and after the runaway pajamas.

Theo didn't even bother to knock on the next door. He ran to it with his pry bar out, ready to go, and broke through in no time.

"There's time," he said to himself.

The flames were beginning to find themselves on the walls and into the ceiling above him. It was too hot to think straight. *Two more apartments.* He smashed through the second door. It was completely empty. There was no furniture. No decorations. It was a vacant room.

"Dammit!" Theo said. His walkie talkie hissed to life. The captain was not happy.

"Get your ass outside! This building is done! You are out of time in there!"

Theo ignored him.

"There's time," he said to himself.

He ran to the last door, kicked it in and was instantly hugged by an oversized dog. He held the dog and looked around to find two small children staring at him from under a blanket on the ground. It was a boy and a girl, maybe eight and ten years old. Theo ran to them and kneeled down beside them.

"Is your mom or dad home? Anyone?" he asked them. They both nodded no. "Come on!" He grabbed the smaller boy and ran to the window. He motioned them away from the glass as he broke through. The wind from the hole in the window immediately ignited more flames behind them. He stuck himself out the window to signal the ladders below. The rest of the crew saw him and immediately sprang into action, moving the aerial ladder toward him. The smoke began to fill the apartment and Theo took off his mask and held it to the young girl's face. Another crew member met him at the top. Theo handed him the small boy first, then the girl, and then the dog.

The flames were everywhere now, and Theo could see nothing but red and the light through the dirty window. He reached out for help onto the ladder when the floor came loose beneath him. He gave one last jump through the window and held onto the frame hard. His pry bar came loose and fell five stories below him.

They moved the ladder closer to him, and another firefighter reached out to grab him. They held one hand out and made a connection, swinging his weight to the top of the ladder. The ladder started to lower, with Theo hanging there, legs dangling in the air. There was a sense of relief that came over the crew.

The ladder rotated away from the building, but one more explosion blasted through the window next to Theo forcing his grip to let up, and he fell two stories to the ground. He landed on his feet, but the force broke his knee and ankle. His doctor told him three months' recovery. He hadn't worked in five.

******

Theo flipped a burnt pancake onto a paper plate and slid it down the counter to his daughter.

"YES!" she bellowed and put her tablet down.

Theo picked up the tablet. "You know, when I was a kid," he began, "I didn't have these fancy-dancy things to play on. I had to actually go outside, and you know what the only toys I had were?"

"Rocks and sticks," Saylor said as she blew on a steaming bite of pancake.

"How'd you know that?" Theo asked.

"You tell me that all the time," she answered.

"Oh… well yeah! That's right. We only had rocks and sticks to play with. And you know what? We were better off for it! We didn't have pancakes either! You know what we had to eat for breakfast?"

Saylor sighed. "Rocks and sticks," she said again.

"That's right. We had to eat rocks and sticks for breakfast," Theo said as he cut into a pancake for himself. They were a little too dark and a little too crispy.

"Ugh… These aren't great," Theo said in disgust.

"Dad, no! They're better than Mom's!" Saylor said. She wasn't a good liar, but she was a sweet liar, and that counted for something.

The two of them ate burnt pancakes together and enjoyed the morning. After breakfast, Theo loaded up the truck with boxes and trash bags of odds and ends that were to be donated. He looked across the street again. There was still no sign of Heather's car.

FORTY-ONE

Al arrived at the late Abner Beckett's house with a paper bag full of groceries and a bottle of wine. The sun was setting as Theo met her at the door. He smiled and took the groceries while leading her inside. Saylor was setting up a game of Battleship at the dinner table. Theo, however, was confident that he was going to win, ever since his daughter recently discovered that you could spell out the word "hi" with the pieces. It was now her go-to Battleship design.

"Saylor, you remember my friend, Al," Theo said to his daughter.

"Hi... oops," Saylor said as she scrambled to cover up whatever clue to her Battleship formation she may have just given away. "I mean... hello."

"Hello again," Al smiled.

Theo popped open the bottle of red wine with a well-hidden struggle. He poured two glasses and handed one to Al as he sat down and joined the two at the table. They laughed and played round after round of Battleship. Theo played some of his father's old records. It was a great remedy to the day before.

Theo checked his phone. "Holy cow, it's time for bed," he said.

"Awwww," Al and Saylor said in unison.

"Oh, don't you two join forces against me," Theo said. "Alright, let's move it. Sweet dreams and flying machines. Toothbrush!"

Saylor got up and went in to brush her teeth. She came back out and gave Theo a hug before heading off to bed. "Goodnight," she said.

"Goodnight, kiddo," Theo answered. Saylor headed off to the bedroom and hopped in bed.

"She's a sweet kid," Al said.

"Takes after me," Theo said.

"I'll bet," Al joked.

"Want to get some air?" Theo asked.

"Sure."

Theo held the door to the backyard open, and the two stepped out into the fresh air. Frogs were singing in the distance. The fireflies were almost gone for the year, but a few held on to poke tiny lights in the darkness.

The old backyard had seen better days. There were tufts of grass growing through the cracks of the concrete patio. An empty bird feeder hung from a small tree. Theo remembered being a kid and watching the squirrels rob blind those innocent sparrows. The fence had been broken for years, and left a gap that led into a giant dark field.

Al walked over and gave Theo a kiss. They embraced, and Theo held her close in the cool air.

"I had fun tonight," Al said.

"Me too." Theo smiled. He felt conflicted again. Surely you aren't supposed to meet someone while at home for your father's funeral? It seemed out of place, yet Theo couldn't help but feel like he was right where he was supposed to be.

Something whizzed by them. Had it not been for the loud smack into the wooden siding behind them, they may have never even noticed it.

"What the hell was that?" Theo said. He let go of Al and turned to investigate the sound. There was a short arrow sticking out of the house. The knock was illuminated by a small LED light.

"Is that… an arrow?" Al asked.

Theo looked out into the darkness.

"Yeah…," he answered.

"Should we maybe go inside?" she said again. Another arrow whizzed between the two and hit the wooden siding behind Theo.

"YEAH!" Theo said.

They broke into a run toward the door. A spotlight hit them from the other side of the yard.

"DON'T TAKE ANOTHER STEP YOU FLY-EATING BAG OF SHIT!"

Theo and Al both stopped and raised their hands into the air. Huckleberry Gary stepped into the light with his pink crossbow pointed at Theo.

"Gary?" they both yelled in unison.

"Miss, you can step away from this monster. I'm not here for you," Huck said.

"YOU COULD'VE KILLED US!" Al yelled at him.

"Actually I just saved your life," Gary responded, "Move away from the reptile, please." He motioned with his crossbow. Al moved a few steps away, lowering her hands.

"What the hell are you doing?!" Theo asked him.

"You shut your mouth, you shape-shifting bastard! I've finally got you," Huck told Theo. There was contempt in his voice.

"Shape-shifting?" Theo thought maybe he didn't hear him right.

"That's right," Huck said. He turned to Al. "Ma'am, I hate to tell you this, but you were just smooching with an illuminati reptilian shape-shifter."

"What is he talking about?" she asked Theo.

"Illuminati. David Icke. Reptile people." Theo sighed.

"Bingo. I saw you in the woods! Near the motel. I saw you in the woods after the bar! I finally got you now," Huckleberry Gary said. He pointed the crossbow at Theo.

"PUT THE WEAPON DOWN." Another voice came from the darkness. An older man approached slowly with a six-shooter revolver drawn. Theo recognized Dino and felt a moment of relief.

"Oh, thank God. Detective Perez, I'm so glad you are here," Theo said as he lowered his hands.

"You keep your hands in the air," Dino said to Theo, keeping his gun drawn on Huckleberry Gary. "You're under arrest, Theo."

"What?!" Theo put his hands back up. "Wait, aren't you retired? You can't arrest me."

"Jesus… Let's call it a citizen's arrest," Dino answered.

"I didn't think that was a real thing," Al said.

"Oh, believe me, it's real," Huckleberry Gary added. "I do it all the time."

"I'm being citizen's arrested? For what?!" Theo asked.

"For the murder of Dr. Anderson, the murder of Gwen Jones, the murder of Suzi Hendrix…"

"Wait… murder of Suzi Hendrix…?" Theo felt a sense of dread creep up.

"And the murder of Gustav… an innocent pet turtle," Dino added.

"What kind of sick son of a bitch kills a child's pet turtle?" Huck said, shaking his head with disgust.

"Actually, it was a fifty year old man's pet turtle," Dino said.

"What kind of a sick son of a bitch kills a fifty year old man's pet turtle?" Gary said again, still shaking his head in disgust.

"A sociopath, that's who," Dino answered. He looked at Gary. "Gary, put down that damned crossbow."

Huckleberry Gary lowered his pink weapon. He stared Theo down as he pulled out his flask and took a swig.

"You said Suzi Hendrix… She is dead?" Theo asked.

"Don't play dumb with me," Dino said. "Put your hands behind your back." Dino approached Theo, holstered his revolver and took out his cuffs.

"Good God, people," Theo said as Dino cuffed him. "This is all a crazy, weird misunderstanding. Gary, if I'm a reptile, why would I kill a turtle? Why would I kill one of my own? That doesn't make much sense, does it?"

"Turtles are amphibians!" Huck answered.

"No they're not. I'm pretty sure they're reptiles." Theo looked at Al. "Right?"

"I'm not sure, to be honest," she said.

"Yeah, I'm pretty sure they're amphibians," Huck said.

"I think amphibians do live in both aquatic and terrestrial habitats," Al said.

"Like a turtle!" Huck said.

"I feel like that's wrong, but I just don't know enough about turtles," Theo said.

"GODDAMMIT!" Huck said. "It doesn't matter. It's not even a rule that reptiles don't kill reptiles anyway! This is just more of your illuminati mind games." He pointed the crossbow at Theo again.

"So you're agreeing that turtles are reptiles?" Theo asked.

"SHUT THE HELL UP!" Dino interrupted. "Jesus Christ! Turtles lay hard-shelled eggs on land. They're reptiles. For crying out loud, lower the damned crossbow, Gary." Dino began walking Theo toward the side of the house.

"Wait! You can't just take him to jail!" Huckleberry Gary kept his crossbow pointed at them. "I'm sorry, detective," he said, "but if I let you take him in, he's just going to escape. I can't let him go! I've worked too long to let him go now."

"What the hell are you talking about?" Dino said.

"Illuminati. David Icke. Reptile people," Al answered.

Dino led Theo by the handcuffs toward the front of the house. Gary kept his crossbow aimed at them and followed. Dino moved slowly into the driveway next to his car.

"I can't let him leave." Huckleberry Gary warned the retired detective.

"Gary, I'm taking him in," Dino said as he opened the back door to his sedan. "Your lizard hunt does not transcend the law."

Huckleberry Gary felt the anger enter him. He had spent countless hours of his life in service to this community. This was his moment. He was the defender of Kenton, and the Illuminati was about to get away, again. Time was running out. Gary acted.

He took aim toward the sedan and fired a bolt into the back tire. It deflated with a loud hiss almost instantly.

"Goddammit Huck!" Dino yelled out. He unholstered his six shooter and pointed it at Gary. "There's a spare in the trunk. Change it. Now," he said.

Before anyone could react, glass shattered from the other side of the house. They all turned and looked toward the commotion. There was a scream.

"SAYLOR!" Theo yelled.

FORTY-TWO

Panic poured into Theo like water through a broken dam as he broke free from Dino. Dino didn't fight back, and they all ran inside the house. The glass door that led to the patio was completely shattered.

Theo dashed down the hallway toward the bedroom where Saylor was sleeping, only to be hit in the chest and knocked on his back. He couldn't believe his eyes when he saw the monster standing over him. Water dripped from the creature and landed on Theo's face. It smelled like silt and fish. He looked over to see that the bedroom had been closed, but there were breaks in the wooden door. The monster had broken it trying to get to his daughter.

The monster kicked Theo hard and sent him rolling across the floor and back into the kitchen where the rest of the crew stood in shock.

Dino unloaded his pistol into the creature; the bullets went through him like mud. One shot struck the knee which seemed to slow the monster down a little bit as it began toward them.

"Suck on this you fucking...." Huckleberry Gary couldn't think of anything to say as he fired his crossbow. The bolt hit the monster through the chest. The red LED knock on the end of the bolt glowed in the creature where its heart should be.

The monster grabbed the dinner table and threw it at them, knocking them all back. Theo managed to stand up, but with his hands still handcuffed behind him he had nothing else to try but to head-butt the creature in the face. The creature stumbled slightly before head-butting Theo in return, sending him to the ground again. He looked back into the hallway and saw Saylor sneaking out.

"HEY!" Theo yelled at the monster getting its attention, hoping to distract it from his daughter.

Al ran to Saylor, picked her up, and they took off out the front door. The monster noticed this and gave Theo another kick, but before he could turn to give chase, Huckleberry Gary jumped on its back and stabbed it in the neck with his knife. The creature tried to shake the navy man off of him resembling some kind of freaky rodeo. Dino helped Theo to his feet, and they ran outside.

The bay windows in the front room were smashed to pieces as Huckleberry Gary was thrown through them and into the front yard, landing at Dino's feet. He let out a painful groan, as Dino helped him up. The monster followed through the jagged window frame ripping its old tattered sleeve completely off revealing its shoulder. He landed with a thud behind the group.

Dino stood between the group with his arms out, acting as a barrier between them and the creature. He closed his eyes and braced himself.

Headlights appeared out of nowhere, lighting the monster up before smashing into it and driving through the yard and straight into the front of the house, coming to a stop with the rear tires still in the yard. The monster lay pinned underneath the wreckage. Abner's old sofa sat upside down on top of the hood. It wasn't going to be a cheap repair.

Heather stumbled out of the driver's seat. Her face was full of shock and anger and sadness. She didn't say anything but walked over and hugged Theo, his hands still cuffed behind his back.

"Suzi..?" he asked. Before Heather could respond, the car began to move slowly. The creature was lifting it up and trying to escape.

"We need to move!" Dino said.

"The truck," Theo answered. He, Saylor and Al climbed into the cab. Al jumped behind the wheel. The rest of the crew jumped into the rusty old bed.

"The keys are in my pocket!" Theo said to Al. She fished them out, started the engine, and put it in drive. They drove through the front yard and into the roadway speeding through a four way stop.

Saylor grabbed her dad and held on tight. She had tears in her eyes. Theo put his cheek on top of her head.

"What the hell is that thing?!" Theo yelled out the back window.

"I've been wondering about that for a long time. Apparently, it's not you," Dino yelled over the wind, leaning into the cab. They drove in silence for a minute.

"Where are we going?" Al said.

"We need to go to the police station," Dino responded.

"No," Theo said, "I know where we need to go to get some answers. Head south toward Fall Creek. I'm sorry, but this night's only going to get weirder for you guys."

FORTY-THREE

Al pulled the old truck over at the bridge to the hidden grove and jumped out. Dino helped Huck and Heather out of the truck bed. Theo walked over to Dino with his hands behind his back.

"Am I still under arrest or CAN WE TAKE THESE OFF NOW?!" Theo said as he turned his back toward Dino and shook the cuffs. Dino pulled the keys from his pocket and took the cuffs from his hands. Huck approached Theo and offered his hand.

"Hey, uh… sorry for earlier… you know… with the whole… crossbow…," Huck said.

"YOU ALMOST SHOT US WITH A CROSSBOW!" Al interrupted.

"He tried to shoot you with a crossbow, Dad?" Saylor asked.

"Yes, but lucky for us he has a terrible aim," Theo said, answering his daughter.

"I have an incredible aim." Huck was offended.

Theo grabbed a flashlight from the glove box and led the crew over the bridge and into the darkened grove. It was quiet this time of night. The sun had been set for two hours, and the nocturnal creatures were clocking in.

Everyone sat down next to the water and began to process what had just happened. Theo went to the water's edge and looked for his friend. He saw some movement in the water a few feet away from him. There was a catfish swimming around.

"Mr. Jones," Theo said toward the water. The fish just ignored him. "Mr. Jones!" he said again; still, no response. Theo began splashing the water around. The rest of the gang began to wonder what was going on.

"Theo...," Heather said. "Come on. What are you doing?"

"This is Mr. Jones. This is the catfish I was telling you about," Theo said. "But he's being a dick right now!" He splashed the water with more force. "DUDE! You are embarrassing me," Theo said.

"I think he's lost it." Heather was nodding her head.

"Theo, come on. Let's sit down," Al said as she grabbed him by the arm.

"Hold on," Theo said, refusing to go along with her. "He's right there," he said, pointing at the water. "Maybe if I throw some rocks in there... he hates that though. It's like Pompeii."

The gang began to look at Theo with sympathy. Theo ignored them and kept splashing some water around.

"What are you doing?" A voice came from across the small pond. Mr. Jones' head was shining in the moonlight. He dipped into the water and swam toward Theo and the rest of the group. They couldn't believe what they were seeing. Mr. Jones popped his head back up.

"Were you just talking to that other catfish?" he asked.

"I… I'm sorry. I thought it was you!" Theo answered.

"You thought that uggo was me?! What the hell, man? How could you confuse him with me? I'm a goddamn Adonis compared to him." Mr. Jones couldn't believe what he was hearing.

"You're a catfish, he's a catfish… How am I supposed to tell the difference?" Theo offered.

"Oh, we all look alike? Is that what you're saying?" Mr. Jones demanded.

"All catfish?" Theo said. "Yes, you all look alike. All catfish look the same to me."

"Wow, okay," Mr. Jones said. "That's racist, man."

"What?!" Theo said.

"Dad… do not be a racist," Saylor said.

"I'm not a racist!" Theo defended himself.

"I'm sorry to interrupt here," Dino jumped into the conversation. "But what in the ever living fuck is going on? Who are you? What is this? Am I having a stroke?"

"Do you smell burnt toast?" Mr. Jones asked.

"This is my weird, slimy catfish friend, Mr. Jones," Theo said. "And to be honest, I don't understand it either."

"For the last time, I'm not slimy!" Mr. Jones said. "It's a thin layer of mucus. I've told you.., it's antimicrobial… there's enzymes and shit in it. It's not slime! It's just normal fish stuff."

"Unbelievable," Heather said.

"Jonesy look, we just had a pretty bad night. The monster came to the house," Theo said. "It tried to kill us. We need some answers."

"Oh my gosh," Mr. Jones said. "I was hoping it wasn't true…"

"What isn't true? What is going on?" Theo said.

"It's back. The monster that Abner and I stopped…," Mr. Jones said.

"What is it?" Theo asked.

"I wish I could just show you, Theo. I only have one trick left," Mr. Jones said.

"I'd say that a murderous river monster trying to kill me is a good reason to use that trick," Theo said.

"No, no, no. Theo, it wasn't trying to kill you," Mr. Jones said. "This monster, it doesn't kill you. This monster was made out of pure rage and hatred. It goes after whatever it is you love the most. That's how it gets stronger."

Theo looked over at Heather. She had a tear in her eye. He looked over at his daughter. *What you love the most?* The monster was after her.

"Besides," Mr. Jones continued, "I can't show you, I only have one trick left. That's it. I can't use my last trick… Then I'm out of tricks."

"And if you run out of tricks..?" Theo asked.

"Then… I'm out of tricks," Mr. Jones answered.

"What does that mean?!" Theo demanded an answer.

"He'll die," Al said. Mr. Jones looked over at Al.

"Damn, Theo," he said, "Is this your date? She's hot! Whoa! I'm sweating!" He swam a few feet closer to where Al was standing. "Hey, what's up?" Mr. Jones said in a lowered voice. "I'm Mr. Jones. You are an absolute beauty. Cookies on Christmas. What's your sign?"

"Stop," she said.

"Jones, you said something before about bad magic in this river? Something about the Villa Leila," Theo said in an effort to stay on track.

"Yes, right. Something very bad happened up there, at the same moment something very good happened right here. Do you guys know the story behind Villa Leila?" Mr. Jones said.

"Sure, the rich guy built it for a woman he loved. She never arrived, and he died. Something like that," Dino added.

"I know the story," Saylor jumped in. "It was Gray Dougal, the wealthy artist cat. He fell in love with a woman named Leila in Morocco. Her dad was a barber. They ran away together, and Gray and Leila split up to keep her safe. She went with his best friend, Carson. They planned to meet here, but Leila never came home, and he lived alone for a few years before dying of a broken heart. Also, he had a dog named Cheddar, and he still roams the grounds."

Theo put an arm around his daughter and smiled at her.

"You're right," Mr. Jones said. "Cheddar, the ghost dog, does still wander the grounds! But there's more to the story than that. You see, Leila did find her way to Kenton... only it was years later. And Gray Dougal didn't die of a broken heart... He was murdered..."

FORTY-FOUR

"It was spring of 1985, arguably the best year for the arts," Mr. Jones began as everyone gathered around to listen.

"That's so not true it's not even worth the conversation," Theo interrupted.

"I said 'arguably!'" Mr. Jones said. "Anyway… it was 1985, and Gray Dougal was in the pit of an existential crisis," Mr. Jones continued. "One afternoon, Gray was just waking up from his usual morning nap when he noticed that his dog was not at his usual spot near the wood burning stove.

'Cheddar!' he yelled through the small empty castle. But Cheddar was nowhere to be found.

It had been nearly ten years since Gray had made it back home to Kenton. Ten years of waiting for Leila. See, after Gray split off from the two in the desert, Carson and Leila were supposed to head north and catch a boat to Spain, but Carson had other plans.

You see, he had fallen in love with Leila too. And his jealousy for Gray had only grown stronger. He had decided to go behind Gray's back and tell Leila's father about their plans to run away together."

"Wow," Saylor said.

"So," Mr. Jones continued, "instead of heading to Spain, Carson took Leila back to her home and ended up staying in Morocco to continue working for Leila's father. He knew that Leila was never going to stay there, and even if she did, eventually Gray would return to find her. So, Carson did the only thing he could think of. He lied to her. He decided to forge some letters. He had one sent to Gray's family in Kenton, saying that Leila had died on their way to Spain. He had another fake letter sent to himself from Gray's family that said Gray had died in an accident. When he showed Leila the letter she was devastated. Her heart would never be the same. When Gray's family gave him the news, he didn't leave the villa for nearly a year."

"Then what?" Saylor asked the catfish. She was sitting next to Theo on the bank of the pond.

"Over time, Carson eventually worked up the ladder in Leila's father's fruit export business. He made a deal with him to marry Leila, that bag of shit!"

"Come on, man," Theo said, motioning toward his daughter, "Language."

"It's okay, Dad. I've heard those words on YouTube," Saylor said.

"What's YouTube?" Mr. Jones asked.

"It's a place where all kinds of people are consistently marginalized," Theo said. "So what happened next?"

"Right. Where was I?" Mr. Jones said.

"Gray was looking for his dog," Al answered.

"Yes, exactly. So Gray woke up from a nap and couldn't find his dog! He looked all around the house, and then he saw him outside his window. There was a woman in the driveway petting him.

He walked outside and called Cheddar before he realized who it was! It was Leila. He froze in place and was completely shocked.

'Leila..,' Gray said.

'I thought you were dead!' she answered as she ran to him and hugged him.

He held her for a moment and leaned back to look her in the eyes.

'You're alive,' he said. He couldn't believe what he was seeing.

'Carson... He told me you were dead,' she said, tears beginning to well up in her eyes.

'I was until this moment,' he said."

"Awww," Saylor and Al said in unison. Huckleberry Gary gave an eye-roll to Dino. Dino nodded in agreement before turning his head to wipe away a tear.

"I don't actually know what they said to each other. I'm just using my creative license," Mr. Jones said. "What can I say? I'm a gifted storyteller. Anyway..," the catfish continued, "Gray held Leila tight. She was older and felt stronger. Ten years of feeling lost, hoping that he could just let it go, and open himself up for love again, but now so glad he didn't.

'How...?' Gray said into the dark hair pressed against his cheek. He couldn't find the words. She wiped the tears from her cheek and pulled out a newspaper clipping from her purse. It was a picture of Gray from last year at a community fundraiser.

See, Carson was a clever bastard, but even clever bastards make mistakes once in a while. In an effort to ward off the occasional homesickness, he would have copies of the Kenton newspaper mailed to him once in a while, and this edition just happened to have an article about a local fundraiser. Who was in the background of the photo? Why, it was Gray and his dog, Cheddar! Leila knew that she had been lied to.

Gray was alive! So one night she snuck away under the stars and made her way to Kenton with the hope of finding her long lost love. A love that found its way all thanks to a small town chili cook-off. I don't even like chili!

Things were great for a short while, but they both knew that Carson was inevitably on his way for them. It's hard to say if it was Carson's obsession with Leila, or his hatred for Gray that drove him, but eventually he came to the Villa Leila.

It was evening, and Gray and Leila were lying together on a couch listening to music. There was a loud knock on the door that echoed throughout the small castle. Gray answered the door but before he saw who it was, he was hit over the head by the handle of a revolver."

"Was it raining out?" Al asked. "It seems like it should be raining out."

"Of course it was raining out!" Mr. Jones answered. "Thunder was rumbling in the distance, too!"

"Awesome," Al said.

"Gray hit the floor hard. Carson stepped over him with his revolver pointed at Leila," Mr. Jones continued.

"'Hello, Leila,' Carson said to her as he walked through the door. Leila was still sitting on the couch and put her hands in the air. Carson pointed the gun back at Gray on the floor. Leila pleaded with him not to shoot. Carson pointed the gun back at her.

'Shut up!' he yelled at her. He was wearing a tailored suit with leather satchel slung over his shoulder. Water dripped off of his chin from the rain! Just then, Cheddar came out of nowhere and bit him in the arm! Carson dropped his gun. Gray kicked him in the legs and the two began to fight. Leila ran up the stairs. Carson punched Gray hard in the jaw and he smashed through the coffee table. It was nuts! I'm pretty sure Gray threw a whip kick."

"What's a whip kick?" Dino asked.

"It's a taekwondo kick. Pretty standard," Huck answered.

"I doubt Gray Dougal used a whip kick," Theo said.

"If he was trained in taekwondo he might have," Huck argued. "That's what I would have done probably."

"Okay. Did Gray know taekwondo?" he asked Mr. Jones.

"How should I know?" Mr. Jones answered.

"Okay," Theo said while rubbing his temples. "Then what happened?"

"Carson got out of the struggle and ran up the stairs and after Leila, who had run out onto the roof. Gray followed, grabbing Carson's legs and slowing him down. They fought each other up the stairs. Carson pulled a knife and stabbed Gray in the stomach. Gray screamed out in pain and rolled away. Carson stood up and followed Leila out onto the roof.

He and Leila faced each other as Gray slowly made his way to stand between her and his old friend. Blood was soaking through his shirt. They could see the storm clouds in the distance over the mighty Mississippi River. Carson held the ornate knife out toward them.

'You LIED to me!' Leila screamed at Carson.

'How is this happening?!' Carson yelled back at them.

'She figured out your lies, Carson,' Gray said. 'Why did you do it?'

'This wasn't supposed to happen,' Carson answered. 'You have everything! You weren't supposed to win. I don't understand how this happened!'

'Win?! I didn't win anything! We used to be friends! How could you do this to us?!' Gray asked again.

Carson held open the satchel with his other hand and pulled out a dusty oil lamp. He threw it on the ground in front of them. Gray recognized the old relic.

'What was your wish?!' Carson asked him.

'Where did you get that?!' Gray ignored his question.

'Answer me!'

'You went back to the cave?! You stole him?'

'Tell me!' Carson stepped closer with his knife toward him. Lightning cracked through the sky. It started to rain even harder!

'If you had this... why not just get whatever you wanted? Why do all of this?' Gray asked.

'You don't get it. We both found it. It takes us both to make it work!'

Before Gray could respond, Leila jumped at Carson and attacked him. They fought, but she was no match for him. Carson slammed the knife into her chest. Life began to leave her eyes as she sank to the rooftop.

'NOOOOO!' Gray screamed in panic. He ran to her and held on to her tight, desperately trying to hold captive the fleeing life inside her, but it was pointless, like trying to plug a broken damn with a toe. Her eyes made their way to his, and he watched the love of his life drift away. Ten years to find her, only to have her taken again.

Rage seared into Gray as he dove into Carson. Carson swung the knife at Gray but missed, slamming the blade into the concrete barrier on the edge of the roof. The blade cracked as it sliced into Carson's own hand. Gray threw him to the ground and began to beat him.

'You goddamn fool. My *wish..*,' he yelled through the rain, 'was for you to finally find some peace in this world!' Gray quit punching him. He was winded and lost and slumped against the edge of the roof.

Peace? Carson couldn't believe his ears. 'You're a liar,' he said.

'You were my best friend!' Gray said to him.

Carson stood up, and something else took over him. He was nothing but pure hatred now. There were no other emotions left. Just pure, dark, unstoppable hatred. He dove into Gray, and they slammed into the rooftop barrier, the only thing between the wild river below them, down the edge of the bluff. Carson grabbed Gray around the neck and began to strangle him. Gray looked over at Leila's body and knew there was only one thing left for him in this life. He had one purpose now. He used all of the strength that was left in him to push himself up and over the edge, taking Carson down with him. The two crashed down the side of the bluff, and into the dark water, never to be seen again," Mr. Jones said, ending that chapter of the Villa Leila.

The gang sat for a moment trying to make sense of the story they were just told. Theo had his arm around his daughter. Dino was looking up over the trees and to the top of the bluffs in the distance. The historic villa was lit up in the dark night.

"So whatever is going on," Dino said, "must be connected to that place. I think that's where we need to go. Maybe the answer to this bad magic is there."

Theo stood up and helped his daughter to her feet.

"Well, what are we waiting on?" he asked.

"Theo," Dino said. "We need to get Saylor to the police station. Somewhere where she is safe."

"She's safest with us. She's not leaving my side," Theo said. He and Saylor headed toward the trail up the bluffs. The rest of them followed.

FORTY-FIVE

The gang hiked their way up the dirt trail and onto the grounds of the Villa Leila. The randomly placed spotlights lit up the masterpiece, illuminating the periwinkle blue spirals that led up to the cone top tower. A sideways crescent moon reached up from the opposite tower, looking like some sort of celestial horns on the tower's head. It was a beautiful piece of work.

What was once a large field with grass and a garden was now a small parking lot for the part-time history buff looking to kill some time on their business trip to Kenton. In the distance from the bluff, a dirty barge crept up the Mississippi, its lights rippling through the water.

The wind picked up and it was starting to get colder. "What is it we are looking for?" Theo asked.

"I'm guessing we will know it when we find it," Dino answered.

"Perfect," Theo responded.

Huckleberry Gary stopped walking to put his crossbow to his feet, pulling it back and cocking it. He wanted to be ready.

"Please be careful with that," Theo said, motioning toward his daughter.

"Theo, I'm a trained weapons expert," Huck said.

"What are those?" Al asked as she walked by, pointing to two wooden sticks placed in his belt.

Huckleberry looked at her, astounded and scoffed. "These? These are my nunchaku," he said. "It's an ancient weapon that focuses on mobility, speed, and focus."

"Nunchucks?" she asked.

"Yes, some people call them nunchucks. I'm a trained nunchakuka. We know them from their proper term: nunchaku," Huck said.

"First of all, everyone calls them nunchucks," Al answered. "And did you do karate or something? How did you learn nunchuck skills?"

"I would rather not talk about it," Huck said.

"You learned from YouTube, didn't you?" she said.

"Can we just focus on the task at hand?" Huck responded. "We have a mystery to solve, okay?"

"Holy shit, she's right. You learned nunchucks from YouTube," Heather added.

"It was a series of online courses," Huck said.

"It was YouTube videos!"

"We live in the golden age of communication! YouTube is just another platform that they can be found on! It doesn't cheapen it in any way. I have training, goddamn it!"

Huck stormed off toward the front of the group. For a brief moment, Heather forgot about her anguish from losing Suzi. The two women shared a small laugh, and continued toward the castle. Saylor walked next to Huck.

"I think nunchucks are cool," she said to the man.

"Thank you, darling." Huck said. "They're called nunchaku, though."

The field lights illuminated the small castle as they neared the front door. There was a large glass covered box at the entrance that held various information on the history of the home and the story of Gray Dougal and his affluent family. Visiting hours were well over by this time of night, and the doors were locked up.

"You're the cop," Theo said to Dino. "How do we get in? I'm not looking for a breaking and entering charge. Can't you like... jimmy the lock or something?"

"I'm retired," Dino answered. "And no, I can't 'jimmy the lock.' But I do like that term. Haven't heard it in a while. Weren't you a firefighter? Didn't you have to kick in doors?"

"We have axes and haligans. Plus, this place isn't on fire. Plus-plus, I don't want to break the door! What if there's an alarm?"

"We could smash a window?" Huck said.

The three of them argued back and forth for a moment but were quickly interrupted by the sound of the door opening from the inside. Al stepped through it.

"There's no glass in some of these windows," she shrugged. Theo was impressed. He liked her.

They entered through the lobby area and passed the front desk. There was a container for donations next to some pamphlets. Theo made a mental note to come back and give a little for the trouble.

Through the doorway they found the main room with a small gazing pool that had recently been filled in with concrete. The historical society couldn't justify the risk of some random tourist looking at their phone and falling in, breaking an ankle. The pool was surrounded by beautiful spiraling pillars. On the opposite wall hung a very large mirror. Its reflection cheated the room's actual size.

The next room was smaller, but had a few bookshelves. Each of them were full of arbitrary knickknacks and trophies from Gray's adventures. There was a small blue and white porcelain monkey, each hand holding a small lamp. There an incredibly delicate looking tea set next to it, which Gray thought he might break if he looked at it too hard. On the shelf above it, framed pictures of Gray and various family members. A bright red chair sat in the corner with a blanket draped over it. The blanket had a desert landscape woven into it with camels and palm trees and the all-too-obvious oasis. A sign read PLEASE DO NOT SIT IN THE CHAIR. Huck lifted his leg and set it on the seat to tighten the laces on his boots.

"Come on, man!" Theo said in a hushed voice motioning toward the sign.

"What?" Huck responded. "I'm not sitting in it?"

"Semantics."

"We need to focus here," Dino whispered, cutting the argument off from the start. "We aren't just on a museum trip here."

"Why are we whispering?" Huck asked.

They were interrupted by the sound of a whining dog from somewhere in the castle. Everyone froze. The whining slowed down, and the sound of a shaking collar echoed through the empty villa.

"That's why we're whispering. Jesus, is there a freaking guard dog in here?" Theo said.

"'A *freaking* guard dog?' You kiss your mother with that mouth?" Huck said.

Theo motioned toward his daughter.

"I think hunting a magic river monster trumps curse word censorship," Huck answered.

"She's nine!"

"Dad, just because you replace the word in the sentence, it doesn't mean I don't know what word you wanted to say," Saylor mentioned.

"You're nine!" Theo said.

"You may as well just say the word instead of making her process it. In a way, you're actually focusing on the curse word more by the simple act of consciously replacing it," Heather said.

"She's right, Dad." Saylor said.

Theo couldn't find the words to counter. *Fuck*, he thought.

"Can we focus on the newest of our problems, the potentially dangerous guard dog?" Al said, getting everyone back on track. "We all heard it right?"

"Cheddar," Saylor said to her father. Theo looked at her with disbelief. This morning he would have easily ruled out the possibility of a haunted castle and a mysterious ghost dog. Tonight, not so much. In fact, it made sense.

"Cheddar?" Dino asked.

"Gray Dougal's dog. Some say the ghost of Cheddar still roams the grounds..," Saylor said in a spooky ghost voice.

"I think we should split up," Dino said.

"No way..," Heather said. "Haven't you guys seen Ghostbusters?"

"Yeah..," Dino said.

"Then you should know that we shouldn't split up."

"I'm not following," Dino said.

"Well, they split up in that hotel, and then Bill Murray gets slimed by green ghost. Slimer. I'm not getting slimed. No way we split up. We stay together," Heather said.

"Her argument is sound," Huck said, as he leaned his crossbow over his shoulder.

Another collar shake reverberated throughout the halls. Theo looked at his daughter. She seemed scared. He put his arm around her shoulder and pulled her close. "Have you ever seen Ghostbusters?" he asked her.

"No," she looked up at him.

"What!? Oh we are having a movie night tomorrow for sure!"

"Is this another old movie?" Saylor asked.

Theo did the math. Wow, that movie was almost forty years old. He was getting there, too. Life was moving by at the speed of, well, life. He thought about a thing he once read on proportion theory. Time seems to go by faster as you get older because each day, each year was just an increasingly smaller percentage of your life. Every passing year was just a thinner and thinner slice of the pie.

He was shaken from his existential tailspin by the sound of another whine. They exited the small room and followed the stairs to the second level. The hallway at the top of the stairs took a sharp left turn and opened up to a small overlook with the now-cemented-over gazing pool below them. There were a few rooms across the way. The moonlight exaggerated the shadows in the grooves of the ornate pillars.

"It's so crazy that he lived in this beautiful place all alone," Al said as she admired an old oil painting in the corner. The canvas stood upon a beat up wooden easel. The painting showed an incredibly detailed image of an oasis in the middle of a desert. Another mysterious shake of a collar broke up the quiet. It was followed by a quiet whimper of a dog.

"Doesn't sound like he did live alone," Theo responded. "Come on."

They continued down the hallway and took another left toward an open door. As they rounded the corner, they finally saw him. Theo put his arms out, and the crew froze in place.

The chocolate lab sat with a big smile on his face. His tongue hung from the side of his mouth as he looked at his new soon-to-be friends eagerly. There was a glowing blue light surrounding him, and he was just transparent enough that Theo thought he could probably walk right through him.

"Ghost dog…" was all Theo could get out.

The dog stood up and shook as though he just got out of a bath. He caught eyes with Heather and smiled.

"…Good dog," Heather said quietly as she began to back away.

The dog darted toward her in the happiest run in the history of runs. His eyes couldn't contain the amount of joy that was in his heart, and his tongue never went back in his mouth. It just bounced off of the side of his face with every bound he took.

"…no, wait!" Heather pleaded.

The dog jumped through the air and landed on top of her, knocking her to the ground beneath it. Glowing drops of drool covered her face as the ghost dog licked her face over and over again.

"Come here, Cheddar!" Saylor said. "Here, boy!"

The dog got off of Heather and walked over to the kid. Saylor gave him a hug and scratched his ears.

"…I've been slimed," Heather said as she lay on her back, defeated.

"We should have split up," Dino said.

"Shut the hell up," Heather answered from the ground.

The dog left Saylor's side, and walked down the hallway before looking back at them.

"I think it wants us to follow him," Saylor said.

Theo looked at his daughter, wearing a proud smile. He put his hand on her head and scuffed her hair a little bit before offering it to Heather to help her up. They watched the glowing labrador as he continued on down the hall and up another flight of stairs, right through the rope barrier that was placed to keep the tourists out. It's amazing what little it takes to herd people away.

The gang followed the dog up the stairs and found themselves in a storage area. The massive room seemed to be the master bedroom at one time, but was now full of old boxes and useless junk. Remnants from the villa's long and empty past. Huck opened one of the boxes to find it full of pamphlets circa 1995. Cheddar circled them before moving to the far corner where he began to paw at a beat up, old box beneath a tower of plastic bins. They followed and pulled the bins down from the top of the box. Theo wiped the dust from the box and wondered just what this ghost dog was trying to show them.

He pulled the dusty flaps open to find it full of random crap. He pulled a few pictures out. It was an old photograph of two kids. There were some newspaper clippings about the villa when it was being built.

"It's just a bunch of Gray Dougal's stuff..," Theo said as he continued sifting through.

The dog broke through and jammed his head into the box. He was searching for something. His tail began to wag ferociously before popping back up with something in his mouth. He brought it to Saylor and dropped it in her hands. It was a baseball.

"Gross," Saylor said as she wiped some glowing drool on her pants.

"What is that?" Theo said.

"It's a baseball," Saylor said as she handed it to him.

Dino grabbed it before Theo could.

"Are you kidding me?" Huck said. "It dragged us up here to dig through all this shit just to play a game of fetch? This is a waste of time. We need to find this thing and put a bolt through its evil, rivery-monster heart."

"There was something written on here, but it's too faded to make out," Dino said, giving the ball back to Theo.

Theo looked closer at the ball. There was some old faded ink.

"First... home..." Theo tried to read the writing. "I don't know." He gave the ball a gentle, underhanded toss. It rolled down the old wooden floor and into another corner next to a bookshelf.

"Go fetch, buddy," Theo said to the Cheddar. The dog just sat there with a look on his face that read something like, "Why would you do that?" He walked over to where the ball landed, walked right through the boxes, like a ghost dog would, picked up the ball, and returned it to Saylor. She gave him a pat on the head, before the dog vanished into a glowing, slobbering mist.

FORTY-SIX

The crew left the storage room with no more direction than when they came. Dino Perez, shedding his usual stoicism, was audibly frustrated, mumbling to himself in variations of Spanglish. No one even brought up how crazy it was that they met Cheddar, the ghost dog. Normally something like that would be a highlight of conversation.

The late night moon was now hidden behind some clouds, and the first floor of Villa Leila was darker than before. The shadows began to play tricks on Huck, and he was on extra alert. "It's quiet," Huck said. "A little… too quiet."

Al scoffed.

"Come on, dude," Heather said.

"What?" Huck said.

"Could you be any more of a cliché?" Al added.

"Exactly," Heather said in agreement.

They heard a car door slam shut from outside the castle walls. Theo signaled for everyone to stay put, and he moved as softly as possible toward an open window that was facing the parking lot. A police officer was shining his flashlight on the villa. Theo could hear the sounds of the walkie-talkie.

"It's the fuzz," he whispered back to the group.

"Must have been a silent alarm," Dino thought out loud.

"We were poking around here for like twenty minutes," Al said. "That's an awful response time."

"We have an evil, murderous river monster poking around town. The cops have been a little busy," Dino said.

"I'll take him out," Huck said.

"What the hell are you talking about?" Theo said. "We aren't going to shoot a cop!"

"Of course not," Huck said. "I'm not a psychopath... I'm going to choke him out. I'll use a sleeper hold, or maybe a reverse guillotine. It depends on his level of training."

"You've got to be kidding me." Theo said.

"No good?" Huck said.

"We aren't going to attack a cop," Dino said. "I'll handle it." Dino moved from the shadows and into the kitchen. He unlocked the door to the back lawn. As he opened the door, another alarm went off. The ring was deafening. Flood lights lit up the grass. The police officer immediately drew his service weapon and moved toward the outer wall. Dino ran back inside to join the group. "My bad, my bad," he said.

Saylor held her hands over her ears. Theo put his hands over hers to help.

"Now what?" he yelled over the high pitched alarm. It was jarring. Theo did not want to get arrested for trespassing, especially in front of his daughter. He could see a custody battle now.

Well, your honor. My ex-husband's idea of parenting seems to be breaking into Moroccan themed castles and stealing random junk with the help of a ghost dog, a drunken, illuminati-reptile-hunter, an old man who happened to put him under arrest earlier, his best friend who is also a pot-head, mind you, and his new girlfriend of two weeks, who is also a little younger than me, which doesn't bother me, but come on... And all because a talking catfish told him there was some clue there on how to defeat a murderous river monster. I'd say that the obvious course of action would be to raise the child support, lower the parenting time, and possibly castrate him.

What do you have to say for yourself, Mr. Beckett?

Well, we didn't actually break in. The window was open. I just want that on the record.

"Listen," Dino said. "We should just go outside, slowly, with our hands up and explain all of this. Huck, you should probably leave your weapons here, though."

"I am a weapon," Huck said.

"I know, big guy," Dino put his hand on Huck's shoulder. "But we should play this one cool."

"Okay, but I don't like it one iota," Huck said as he reluctantly placed his collection of weapons on the ground. They walked out of the door in a line with their hands up. Saylor kept her hands over her ears. Theo kept her behind him.

"We are unarmed!" Dino yelled over the alarm and at the cop.

"Keep your hands in the air!" The police officer moved in front of them with his gun drawn. "I have the suspects lined up. Five adults and a kid. How's it coming with that alarm?" he said into the receiver on his shoulder.

The gang stayed in a line, hands in the air, waiting for an opportunity to explain. The alarm was still going off. The officer was busy talking and in no mood to hear whatever crazy story they were about to give him.

As the officer ignored them, Theo saw something beyond the tree line. A small red light was breaking through the dark. It was faint, and barely there, but getting brighter as it moved closer.

"What is that red light?" Theo said.

Huck knew what it was immediately. "Oh shitness," he said.

Theo didn't need to hear the answer. It was clear now that it was closer. It was the red LED from the light-up knock on the end of one of Huck's crossbow bolts. The same bolt that he had fired into the creature's chest earlier that night. The monster had found them.

FORTY-SEVEN

"Officer..," Theo said with his hands in the air.

"You have the right to remain silent, you know," The police officer answered, facing the crew with his back to the woods. The monster was closing in behind him.

"Yes but…" Theo tried again.

"I'd recommend using it," the police officer said as he lit up a cigarette and took a long drag. The end of it slowly pulsed a bright red resembling the red light that was protruding from the approaching river monster's chest.

"Turn around, man!" Huck said.

"Sounds like contempt of a cop to me," he took another drag. "You feeling disrespectful, buddy? You ever been kneecapped?"

"Of course Bad Lieutenant would show up tonight," Theo put his arms down and pointed behind him. "There's a goddamn river monster coming right for us!"

"A river monster, huh? You punks boofing some drugs tonight? What kind of role model is that for the kid?" the cop said.

"SERIOUSLY TURN AROUND!" Saylor pleaded.

"Listen kid, I don't know what kinda hippy dippy bullshit your family is on here, but I'm the one giving the orders here…"

Before he could finish his sentence, the monster flipped the officer's car. It landed in the yard close to the outer wall of the villa. The windows shattered, sending glass all over the manicured lawn. Gas oozed from the tank forming a small puddle beneath it. He grabbed the cop and power lifted him straight up overhead. The cop let out a raspy scream as the creature threw him twenty feet across the yard and into the leaking car. On impact the cigarette dropped from his hand and ignited the pool of gas. It burned through the yard like a lit fuse and within seconds the car was ablaze.

"RUN!" Theo led everyone back through the kitchen door and into the villa to hide. They ducked into a corner next to the employee refrigerator. Heather snuck off and into the main room. Theo turned to the group.

"I'm going to go and make sure the policeman is okay," Theo said to his daughter.

"No! Don't go out there! Please," Saylor pleaded.

"I'll only be a minute," Theo answered.

"It's out there, though!"

"He's hurt, kiddo," Theo said. "We gotta help him if we can."

"I'll go with you," Dino said.

"Me too," Huck said.

"No," Theo said. "Someone needs to stay with Saylor…"

"I'll stay with her," Al said.

"I'll stay, too," Heather reentered the kitchen with Huck and Dino's weapons. "We'll take care of her." She handed the equipment to Huck.

"You can keep the crossbow," Huck said to her.

"No, I'll keep the nine," she said as she handed it to him. She placed the gun in the back of her black jeans. Just twenty-four hours ago, she had lost the love of her life. She couldn't tell if she was in shock, or if there was some other instinct kicking in, but she was fully focused now. There was no anger or sadness, just pure focus on ending this creature's existence.

Huck couldn't help but have some feelings, too. He was finally part of something that mattered. "Here," he said to Al as he handed her the crossbow.

Theo poked his head out of the door and scoped out the yard. There was no sign of the monster anywhere. The officer was lying in the grass just beyond the flames from the burning car. He couldn't tell if the man was breathing or not.

"Watch my back," he said to the other two.

A familiar feeling crept into Theo. He hadn't been on a call in six months, and the fear and adrenaline found themselves at home. He learned that the fear was his friend. Fear is an ally. All it wants is to keep you alive.

He kept peering into the night around him, but there was no red light. There was no sound but the cracking of the fire. There was nothing. Theo was about twenty yards away from the car when it finally exploded. The boom was deafening. The hot force put Theo on his back. Flaming scraps of cop car flew through the air. One lucky piece of shrapnel made a bull's-eye through one of the open windows of the Villa Leila and landed beneath the curtains of the window.

The flames tickled the fabric before igniting it. Once the curtains went up in flames, it was only a matter of time before the old wood was a part of it, too. A beautiful cabinet full of old ceramics and framed pictures was next. The walls glowed brighter and brighter with a hellish orange. A bookshelf caught and before they knew it, Heather, Al, and Saylor were trapped with no exit into the outside from the backdoor.

"Oh shit," Heather said. "Come on!" She helped Saylor to her feet, and they ran back into the main room, over the top of the cemented in gazing pool, and into the gift shop where Al stopped them both with her arms spread wide.

The creature was standing at the front door, inadvertently blocking their exit. It had yet to see them. It had been distracted by the sounds of the exploding cop car. The ladies backed away with no other option but to go up the stairs. The fire was moving in quickly.

Heather knew that upstairs is probably the worst place you should go in the event of a house fire. However, their choices were to either excuse themselves past the evil river monster or burn up right then and there.

Back outside, Huck was helping Theo to his feet. Dino was busy trying to call in some backup on the downed officer's walkie-talkie, but the explosion took both it and the officer out. He grabbed his phone from his pocket and connected with 911. Theo sat up and saw the beginnings of the house fire cooking through the villa. The flames cast shadows all throughout the lawn; tall, dark specters growing more and more spastic in their movements as the fire kept eating.

"Where's my daughter?!" Theo said.

"They didn't come out yet," Huck answered.

"Fire department is on the way," Dino said as he joined them. "Where's the monster?"

Theo didn't answer. He didn't know anyway. He just ran to the back door and began to push it open. It barely shifted from the fiery debris barring it shut. Huck ran to him and lent him a shoulder, nudging the door open a few inches. Flames poured out into the fresh air. The way in was no good.

Theo looked around for another option. About thirty feet further down the wall was a window that offered an incredible view over the river. It was just low enough for Theo to reach. The window led into a guest room that had never once been used for anything, especially guests.

Theo found a rock and threw it through the old glass. Huck held his hands out for Theo's foot, offering a lift, and Theo fell into the window with an awkward roll. A rogue piece of glass caught his sleeve and cut him deeply through the back of the shoulder. Blood dripped down his arm, but he couldn't tell the difference between it and the warmth from the surrounding fire. So much was invisible to his senses. Everything was numb but his sight, the heat, and the sound of his pounding heart, desperate to make sure his daughter was okay.

"SAYLOR!" he yelled out to no response.

He got low to the ground. Black smoke was building up. Theo made his way to the main room and to the foot of the stairway. He turned to see the monster walking through the flames toward him. Steam was rising from its shoulders. A hit of adrenaline fired through Theo's body, but before he could make his getaway, a gunshot reverberated through the big room.

The bullet hit the monster in the head, knocking him back for a brief moment.

Theo saw Heather standing over the upstairs handrail with the gun pointed down at the monster. Her eyes were a bright white through the soot, dried blood, and smeared makeup. She motioned for Theo to come on. He ran to her as quickly as possible, up to the third floor, and out onto the rooftop where Saylor and Al were looking for a way down without breaking their necks.

"We have to jump," Theo said. No one liked that idea.

"We will break our necks!" Al said.

Theo looked all around. The fire was going to take the roof out at any moment. There wasn't time. He searched the yard. He only saw grass and random solar powered spotlights, illuminating the sidewalk to the front door. On the backside of them were the bluffs that led straight down into the dark river. At the far end of the yard, across from the small parking lot, stood a maintenance shed. Theo saw this and yelled down for help. Huck was still trying to maneuver the back door.

"Huck!" Theo yelled from the roof.

Huck looked up. Theo pointed toward the shed.

"There's got to be a ladder in there!" Theo yelled.

Huck understood and sprinted to the shed. He kicked in the door and searched through the small room. A ladder hung from the wall behind the decades old lawnmower. He grabbed it and returned to the villa, slamming the ladder against the wall without a thought. It extended to the second floor, but not all the way to the roof. Theo was going to have to lower everyone down.

"DAD!"

Theo spun around to see the monster holding his daughter in the corner with no escape. She scrambled backward until her back hit the edge of the roof, with nothing but the dark river hundreds of feet below her. His muddy fingers gripped the rusted knife as he carefully took aim at her heart. Saylor screamed out, and dropped the baseball that she had been clutching since Cheddar gave it to her. The ball gave a few small bounces and rolled into the foot of the monster, the words "FIRST HOME" barely legible and facing up.

The monster gave pause for a moment as though he recognized the ball. He bent over slowly and picked it up. As soon as the ball hit his palm, he remembered.

******

He was back in the summertime. The sun was in his eyes, and the nerves were rushing through him as they do with most twelve year old kids when they are next at bat.

"Go get 'em Carson!" Twelve-year-old Gray Dougal yelled from the bench.

Carson was the new kid in town and didn't have very many friends. His parents thought that maybe it would be helpful to join a Little League and meet some kids his age. Carson didn't object. He loved baseball and was pretty good at it. He met Gray Dougal at their first practice, and they were instantly friends.

Carson took a few practice swings and watched the fastball smoke right by his teammate, Roger, striking him out. There was a faint collection of applause from the few parents that were actually watching the game as Carson approached the plate. He could still feel the anxiety. Nerves are funny that way. They always outstay their welcome.

Stale hotdogs and warm soda floated through the air. The reverberation of cheap steel bleachers sang out as little kids ran across them. Carson choked up on the bat and squared up to the plate. The first pitch blew by him and smacked into the catcher's glove. Strike one. Carson didn't trust his nerves if he were to get to two, so he decided to swing on the next one regardless of where it went.

The pitch came, and he cracked it. The sound popped through the air. Carson lost the ball in the sun and took off running as fast as he could. It wasn't until he got to second base that he heard the crowd's cheers. It had sailed over the fences to give them two runs, breaking their tie and putting them ahead. He couldn't believe it. His team was going crazy on the bench. Gray had the steel fence clenched in his hands and was shaking it like a madman, hollering at the top of his lungs. It was incredible. They welcomed him like a star when he crossed home and joined them back at the bench. Two more innings and the game was theirs.

After the win, Carson was packing his bag into the back of his dad's pickup truck when Gray ran up to him.

"Here you go, buddy!" Gray pedaled up on his bike. His hat was now on backward to avoid flying off in the high speeds of a preteen's Huffy, and he was wearing his backpack from school. He handed Carson the baseball. After the game, Gray had run out behind the field and found the ball in the weeds.

"You smacked it!" he said.

"Oh wow! You found it?" Carson said. "That was my first home run. I was so nervous. Thank you!"

"First home run?!" Gray said, "Well then... we have to memorialize this moment then!" He grabbed a pen from his backpack. He popped the lid off and wrote the words "FIRST HOME RUN" before handing it back to him.

"First home run! See ya tomorrow, buddy," Gray said. He patted his pal on the back and pedaled off. Over the years, it must have ended up getting mixed up with Gray's stuff, as things tend to do when you share dorms, apartments, and tents in the desert for months on end.

******

The monster felt something. It was unfamiliar and difficult but warm, and it moved through his cold veins like freshly drawn bathwater. Carson had awoken from some deep sleep that we would never understand. Somewhere inside the monster, that same nervous kid who loved baseball was fighting to get out.

The creature held the baseball and lowered his right hand. The rusted blade that was fused to him began to let up on its grip. The weapon fell to the ground, and the monster stepped back from Saylor. Theo watched as something was changing within the creature. He saw a man there. The hardened dirt that was caked over the monster was softening. The dark eyes began to lighten. He fell to his knees and looked up at Theo.

Theo didn't know what to say. He opened his mouth to speak, but before anything could come out the roof gave out beneath them, and they all fell together into the burning castle.

FORTY-EJGHT

Whatever air that was in Theo left his body as soon he hit the ground. He was dazed. The fear of Saylor's fate went through him before the pain. He jumped to his feet. Every step was agony. The fire was everywhere. It was climbing the walls. It was floating above him, burning what was left of the ceiling. The smoke made it impossible to see. He got low and crawled through the main room of the villa. Pieces from the roof were falling and widening the opening, giving the smoke somewhere to go. Theo could make out a figure about ten feet in front of him. It was the monster. His daughter was lying on the ground at his feet.

The wall next to the creature began to crumble. The monster bent over, shielding Saylor from the debris with its back. Theo let out a yell, but nothing could be heard over the roaring engine of the fire. After the rubble had fallen, the monster stood up through the dust. Theo watched it lift his daughter from the ground and bring her to him. As it came closer, Theo could see that it had changed. The muddy creature from the Mississippi was no more. Only a man now remained. The tattered clothes still hung loosely and his hair was disheveled. Theo took his daughter from the man's arms and made his way toward the exit.

The gang met them outside. Heather looked into the burning building and saw him. Carson stood in the doorway of the gift shop. He caught eyes with Heather and raised his hand toward her. She stared back, but before he could react, the building came crumbling down on top of him. The man and the monster were dead. After years of haunting the river, of killing without mercy, Carson Reilly found his end in the crumbling ruins of his best friend's house; the namesake of the only woman that they had both ever loved.

Theo set Saylor down on the grass. She was barely breathing. "Hey kiddo," Theo said to her. He shook her a little bit. She didn't respond. Theo felt warmth in her stomach. It was blood. Something had cut right through her in the fall. He began to panic. She was dying.

"Call an ambulance!!" Theo yelled to no one. The rest of the crew had gathered around. Dino grabbed his phone to make the call.

"There's no time," Dino said. "Shit. The fire department should be here soon."

"There's time..," Theo said to himself. He grabbed Saylor and ran faster than he should have been able to, considering his bad knee after falling three stories. He ran through the dark trail into the woods and back toward the grove. He would get to the truck and get her to the hospital. There was time. He could make it in time. Whatever it took. Heather followed. Then Al. Then Huckleberry Gary.

The first responders were already on their way, but Theo knew that he couldn't wait. He had seen the way a stab wound could shut down the organs. The wound went through her chest. Her lung was filling up with blood. She was getting cold. He knew what this meant. Theo was afraid and desperate and running through the dark path back to the water, back to his truck.

"There's time," he tried to convince himself.

The tree line broke, and Theo found himself back in the grove. His knee finally gave out and he lost control. They both fell to the ground. Saylor was blue. Theo checked her pulse but couldn't find it.

"No, no no no..," Theo said as he rolled her over to give her CPR. The wound was still bleeding out. He didn't know what to do.

"What happened?!" Mr. Jones spoke from the water.

Theo began to tremble. He ripped part of his sleeve off to try and cover the wound.

"She's not breathing!" Theo said.

"What?!" Mr. Jones asked.

"Oh God," Theo began to weep. "She's dying!" He picked her up and began limping to the trees. He didn't know what else to do. The rest of the crew caught up to the grove. They stood there, speechless and covered in soot.

"Theo..," Mr. Jones said calmly.

"She..," Theo couldn't bring himself to say it again. Saylor had stopped breathing completely and had turned blue.

"Theo..," Mr. Jones said again. "Bring her here."

"What?" Theo was in shock. "She's.... not breathing," he said. He just stood there with Saylor in his arms.

"Bring her here. Put her in the water, Theo," Mr. Jones said. His voice was soft and confident.

Heather approached Theo and helped him bring Saylor to the bank of the water.

"She's dead," he said to Heather through tears. Heather put her arm on Theo's shoulder. She looked at Saylor. Her skin had a bluish hue. Her arms hung at her side.

"Get in the water, Theo," Mr. Jones said. "Come on."

Theo stepped off the bank and walked into the water. It was cold, but Theo didn't notice. He didn't feel the water as it raised closer to his waist with each step. He walked through the water like he was walking through a void.

"Let her go, Theo," Mr. Jones said. His head was a few feet in front of him.

"I can't." Theo was frozen and staring at his daughter's face.

"You have to trust me," Mr. Jones offered. "Let her go."

Theo held Saylor out and let her float into the water. She began to sink. Mr. Jones said nothing more. He looked at Theo for a moment and then disappeared into the depths of the water. Then it happened.

The water began to bubble and churn. Theo tried to peek into the darkness, but all he could see was the silhouette of Saylor floating lifelessly above a dim light. He saw the catfish darting around through the light, and then there was nothing. Theo felt the muddy bottom of the pond fall out from beneath him, and he quickly sank into black.

FORTY-NINE

Theo found himself underwater and began to swim to the surface. It was far away, maybe fifteen feet. Just as he was getting desperate for air, he broke through the surface. The grove was different. It was daytime. Heather was gone, along with the others that were sitting by the trees. He searched for Saylor in the water. She was nowhere to be found. Theo stood in the water lost and confused. Then he heard laughter.

He turned around to see a man and a woman laughing together underneath the apricot tree.

"Hello?" he asked them, but the couple offered no response. They didn't seem to notice him at all. He began to walk through the water, closer to them.

"Hello?!" he said again. He looked at the couple closer. *Oh my god.* He recognized the woman first.

"Mom..?" he said. She didn't answer. Theo stood there watching.

"Are you ready for this, Abner?" the woman asked the man while rubbing her pregnant belly.

"Are you kidding me?" Abner joked. Theo barely recognized his father as a younger man. "God, yes I'm excited. I'm so ready to be a dad!" Winona smiled at him.

"I can't wait," Abner continued. "I can't wait for the three of us to sit under this tree together and watch the sun go down. Our tree."

He kissed her gently. "Our tree... We have to make sure people know this is our tree! I need to carve our names into it!" he said as he stood up and got out his pocket knife.

"NO! You'll hurt it!" Winona said. "Don't cut into it."

Abner stood with his knife at the ready. He pondered for a moment before folding the knife back up and returning it to his pocket.

"Okay fine, I have a better idea anyway!" Abner said as he sat back down and took off one of his shoes. He pulled the shoelace out of it and tied it around one of the branches. "Come on, give me your shoe!"

Winona laughed. "No!" she said.

"Darling, we have to claim ownership of our tree... Come on now, fork it over," Abner said.

"My shoe will fall off!" Winona said.

"Too bad!" Abner sat down and grabbed her shoe. Winona laughed as he pulled the lace out and tied it on the same branch.

"You're going to have to carry me if my shoe falls off," she said. "I'm a little bit heavier now that I'm walking for two!"

"What if mine falls off?! You may have to carry me!" he responded. They laughed together. He sat back down on the blanket and leaned over facing his wife. "And when little Theo gets a pair of shoes, we will tie one of his laces here, too. This is our tree now."

It began to sprinkle. A storm was coming in from the distance. Theo stood there in complete shock. He couldn't believe what he was seeing.

"Starting to rain," Winona said.

"Good. You could use a shower," Abner said. Winona held back a laugh and smacked him on the leg.

"Let's go, I don't want to get rained on!" Winona said.

"Alright," Abner responded. "But only because I love ya."

"You better love me," Winona said.

"You know it," Abner answered.

"You promise?" Winona asked.

Abner put his left hand over his right side of his chest. "Of course! Scout's honor!" he said.

"Wrong hand, wrong side, buster," Winona and Theo said in unison. His mother rolled her eyes and began to stand. Abner jumped up to help his pregnant wife to her feet.

"What's more romantic than kissing in the rain?" Abner said as he held his wife close.

"Hmmm... I'd say... pickles! Let's go. I gotta *craving*!"

They giggled together like little kids and hurried off through the trees and out of the grove as the storm came pouring in. Thunder rumbled over the Villa Leila in the distance. *This is the moment.* Theo realized what was going on. *A perfect moment. Something very good happened here... Something very bad happened there.* He looked at the castle in the distance. The thought of his young parents leaving. He looked at the shoelaces hanging in the rain. *Magic. Holy Shit.*

Theo felt the swirling of water around him. It began to bubble and churn again. He looked through the rain at the Villa Leila up on the bluffs in the distance before falling again into darkness. There was no up or down, just dark water as he struggled to find his footing. Muddy ground rose up under him, and he stood up breaking back through the surface of the water. Saylor was in his arms.

"Saylor?!" She was lying in his arms. He looked for Mr. Jones. He was gone.

He looked back down at his daughter. She was motionless. There was nothing left in Theo to give. He felt numb. Then she took a breath. Then another. She let out a small cough. Theo wasn't sure how long he had been holding his breath, but he felt it now. He took in air and felt a relief like no other. Saylor opened her eyes and looked at her father.

"Dad?" she said.

Theo laughed through tears. "Daughter," he answered.

Heather jumped into the dark water and helped them both to the edge. They set Saylor down on the bank, and Theo hugged her tight.

"Dad," she said, "you're choking me!"

"I don't care!" Theo said. He let go and looked at her, checking her up and down for any more injuries. "God, I thought I lost you!"

The rest of the crew gathered around to take a closer look at the miracle they just witnessed. Dino gave Saylor a small pat on the back.

"You're a tough kid!" he said to her.

Al joined Theo, and they embraced in a hug. She kissed him on the cheek. Theo was lost in emotions. He turned back toward the water.

"Mr. Jones?" he yelled. There was no answer. He helped his daughter to her feet. "Can you walk?" he asked her.

"Dad, I'm not the one with the busted knee," she answered. Theo smiled. He put his hand on his knee. There was no pain. He gave it a stretch. It felt stronger. It felt good. He couldn't believe it. His knee was healed. *Magic.*

Theo turned to the water again, and again there was still no sign of Mr. Jones. Theo felt a hand on his shoulder. Theo turned his head to find Al standing by him. He gave her an understanding smile. Mr. Jones was gone. The gang walked out of the grove together and jumped into the truck, Theo had never held his daughter's hand tighter.

EJETY

Saylor woke up on a strange couch. It was noon.

"Hello?" she called out to no answer.

She sat up and opened the curtains to find herself looking out across the street at her late grandfather's home. Her father and Heather were in the front yard, looking at the mess of a window. Heather's car was still in the front yard, with Abner's old couch sitting on top of the hood.

She had fallen asleep on the ride home. She and Theo had slept at Heather's after they returned from the grove.

She ignored her shoes and walked across the street barefoot to join them. Heather smiled. She and Al were sitting on the front step of the concrete porch, coffee mugs in hand.

"Wanna cup of coffee, kid?" Heather asked.

"Coffee? I can't believe I actually considered letting you watch my child," Theo said.

"What?" Heather said in defense of the offer. "I started drinking coffee at nine."

Saylor sat down on the porch next to Heather. She was looking at her phone. There was a picture of her and Suzi pulled up. Saylor saw it and gave her a hug. Theo was busy assessing the damage to the house.

"Looks like the resale went down a little bit, huh?" Theo said. "I guess I won't be able to sell for a while. What do you think, Saylor? Vacation home? I suppose we could afford a few more trips to Kenton every now and then." He picked up a couple bricks and carried them to the side of the driveway.

Heather smiled and snuck Saylor a sip of her coffee. Saylor winced at the bitterness.

******

TWO DAYS LATER

It was just after breakfast and the shady grove was quiet. Theo and Saylor walked through the trees in silence, both wondering to themselves if they would find their missing catfish friend, both of them unsure how to even begin to talk about what they went through the last time they were there. The smell of the muddy water worked in three part harmony with the cool breeze and the sounds of the frogs in the distance. Theo pointed to the apricot tree.

"See that tree?" Theo said to his daughter.

"Yes," she answered.

"Did you know that it's *our* tree?" he asked her.

"What do you mean?" she asked.

They walked over to the tree. Theo held the old ingrown shoelaces out to his daughter. "See these?" he said. "These were your grandma's and grandpa's. They've been here since before I was born."

"Wow, they're really old, huh?" she said.

"Hey! They're not *that* old," Theo said.

"That was like another century ago, Dad," Saylor said.

"Only by a technicality. Whatever! That's not the point. The point is…" Theo gave her a smile before tackling her to the ground and playfully wrestling off a shoe. Saylor laughed and tried to run away but it was too late.

"Oh? What do we have here?" Theo said as he pulled out a shoelace from her shoe. He then took off one of his boots and did the same thing. He stood up and tied the shoelaces to the same branch, overlapping his mother and father's, and left them there hanging in the soft breeze.

Theo finally felt like maybe he understood it all. His father loved his mother. His father loved him. Theo loved his father. He loves Saylor. And they all did it in different, beautifully imperfect ways. Maybe that's the point. Love isn't by rote. It isn't something that you can simply saddle and harness. It's wild and free and demands to be ridden bareback, with every aching moment holding on for dear life. Love isn't an action nor is it a tool. It's instinct.

He put his arm around his daughter, and they walked back toward the tree line, but Theo stopped when he felt something. He couldn't place it, but it was there. He turned around toward the water. *Mr. Jones?* He scanned the water for a sign of life, but yet there was nothing. He waited for a moment. Nothing.

Saylor hugged him. He smiled at her and patted her on the head. They left the grove and crossed back over the creaky wooden bridge, then hopped in Abner Beckett's old beat up Chevy. Theo started the stubborn, dirty engine and looked over at his young passenger.

"What do you think?" he asked.

"Hmmm… How about Elton John?" Saylor answered.

"Oh? A little 'Levon' would hit the spot right now. Good call, Daughter," Theo said as he connected his phone to the stereo.

A white cloud of dust scrambled into the air behind them as they set off down the gravel road. It swirled upward and then fell gently back down in a wide blanket, back over the road and into the fields of an imperfect Midwestern America. The sun burned through the sky, and the lazy clouds moved into place offering some welcome shade over Fall Creek. And there, in Abner Beckett's secret fishing hole, as the bugs resumed their journeys and the frogs and birds continued their songs, no one was around to notice the quick flicker of light that reflected off of the tail of a catfish, as it snapped through the surface of the glassy water, leaving behind a small ripple that, like all things, would eventually disappear with time.

The End.

ACKNOWLEDGMENTS

In a way, this story is a love letter of sorts to my hometown of Quincy, Illinois. As a kid, I used to sit in my dad's flat boat and imagine mysterious creatures hiding away in the Mississippi River while we cruised along the old islands. I'm still convinced to this day that there is more in that river than we know.

I want to thank my mother for all of her valuable work in the edits, sharing her love of reading with me, and, most importantly, her endless support and motivation every time I had second thoughts on chasing a life in writing.

Thanks to the folks at the Villa Katherine in Quincy, Illinois, for sharing their knowledge with me, and for their efforts in the preservation of the castle by saving it from demolition over the years. Please check out Friends of the Castle at www.thevillakatherine.org.

Thanks to the Ripple Bar in Duluth, Minnesota. There is a magical table near the window that is very generous. If you bring it a tequila and soda with lime, and wait patiently with your computer open, it will be very kind to you while you sit and write.

Thank you to the independent bookstores that have been so supportive. Especially, those at Zenith Bookstore (Duluth, MN) and Reader's World (Sedalia, MO) and any other stores that go out of their way to support independent writers and artists!

Made in the USA
Middletown, DE
26 February 2023

25542608R00179